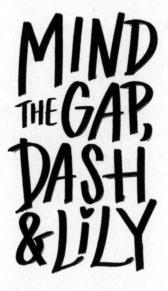

MIND THE GAP, DASH & LILY

ALSO BY RACHEL COHN & DAVID LEVITHAN

Nick & Norah's Infinite Playlist

Naomi and Ely's No Kiss List

Dash & Lily's Book of Dares

The Twelve Days of Dash & Lily

Sam & Ilsa's Last Hurrah

RACHEL COHN &
DAVID LEVITHAN

MIND THE GAP, DASH & LILY

Alfred A. Knopf
New York

THIS IS A BORZOI BOOK PUBLISHED BY ALFRED A. KNOPF

Visit us on the Web! GetUnderlined.com

Educators and librarians, for a variety of teaching tools,
visit us at RHTeachersLibrarians.com

Library of Congress Cataloging-in-Publication Data is available upon request.
ISBN 978-0-593-30153-1 (trade pbk.) — ISBN 978-0-593-30154-8 (lib. bdg.) —
ISBN 978-0-593-30155-5 (ebook)

The text of this book is set in 11.5-point Goudy Old Style Std.
Interior design by Cathy Bobak

Printed in the United States of America
November 2020
10 9 8 7 6 5 4 3 2 1

First Edition

*To all the readers who've made pilgrimages
to the Strand*

one

LiLY

December 21st

I can't be happy unless Dash is miserable at Christmas. It's like it's my job to turn his holiday scowl into a smile.

A happy-looking face doesn't come naturally to Dash. Things that I think should provoke a grin, like a great dog, or cute toddler twins stumbling around a sandbox like drunken pirates, or a rained-on person finally hailing a cab, won't turn his frown upside down. Things that will: a hipster Instagramming their walk through the park and then slipping on that great dog's poo; toddler twins using their yogurt tubes for a sword match that quickly escalates into a not-so-cute food fight involving a lot of sand and angry parents; or a cab discharging an arrogant Wall Streeter directly into an ankle-deep puddle of water.

I don't want to seem like a needy girlfriend, but I kind of live for those rare moments of Dash's smile. It's so pure, maybe because it's so unexpected, and never forced. Dare I say, it could light a whole Christmas tree. (If he heard me say that, it would instantly disappear and threaten never to come back.)

I am determined to bring him some smiles this Christmas. It's too long since I've seen his face, in any expression! He had two great choices last spring before we both graduated high school. He got into Columbia, which would have kept him in New York City and made me very happy, and he got into Oxford University, which, as an Anglophile and a book lover, made him very happy, with the ocean's distance from his parents a big bonus. (They're nice, I guess. But complicated. Not in the fun way.)

Dash and I have been together two years, and although I'm not usually selfless when it comes to letting go of the people or animals I love, I actually encouraged him to go to Oxford. It had always been his dream—he should live it! I deferred admission to Barnard College so I could take a gap year and focus on my dog-walking business and volunteer at my grandpa's assisted living facility. The big bonus for me— for us—and what made the separation feel okay at the time of the big decisions was that I'd have more free time to travel to England to visit Dash since I wasn't in school.

That's how it was supposed to work out, at least. My business grew beyond my wildest expectations and occupied more time than I ever imagined. I haven't seen Dash in person since August. I want to run my hands through his mop of hair, which has grown even longer since he's been studying so hard he hasn't bothered to get it cut. He also hasn't bothered much with shaving. I never thought an unkempt look was my guy type, and it's not just how hard I've been missing Dash—I *like* it. I can't wait to kiss his scruff.

His new life in England is not what Dash expected, either. I've gotten the sense he doesn't like it as much as he thought he would. Or maybe it's Oxford, with all its rules and traditions. Dash is vague about it, but I'm his girlfriend. I sense these things. (His mumbling that maybe he'll look into transferring elsewhere next year was also a clue. I'm not a clairvoyant. I'd like to be, though!)

I figured we'd talk about it more when he came home for Christmas, but a couple of weeks before Thanksgiving, he dropped a bomb on me. He called me for a "talk." The kind that required a text announcing the "talk" ahead of time, so I knew it wasn't going to be a good "talk." Luckily, it turned out not to be the kind of talk that one of our favorite singers, Robyn, suggests some boys have with their girlfriends. Or the "maybe we should see other people" talk. Instead, Dash dropped a Christmas bomb. The I'M GOING TO STAY AT MY GRANDMOTHER'S IN LONDON OVER CHRISTMAS INSTEAD OF GO HOME TO NEW YORK TO BE WITH YOU bomb.

Trigger warning: full-on Lily meltdown.

Deep breaths. Cleansing breaths. Eating feelings.

That's how I kept it together. When I emerged from the

shock, I saw that I had two choices. One, I could rationally accept his decision and spend Christmas at home with my family like every other year, which is the joy of my life, although there would be a lot of missing Dash this year.

I hate being rational.

Or two, I could—

"This was a terrible idea, Lily Bear," my cousin Mark said as we both looked with concern at the wall clock behind his cash register. It was 6:10 in the p.m., or 18:10 as they say in England because I don't know why they talk in military time. "This is not the kind of surprise a boyfriend wants. Especially a snarly one. I shouldn't have said you could crash with us while you waited to spring this on him."

Or two, I could just show up in London as a surprise!

It was a last-minute, spontaneous decision that required a lot of schedule juggling and angry-texting with my mother, whose pre-Christmas plans did not include me sabotaging her expectation that I'd be available round-the-clock to help with cooking, cleaning, and shopping preparations for the big day. But she may have been as relieved as me to get a break from each other. Ever since I decided to put off college for a year, Mom's made it her mission to remind me that my gap year is "just a *temporary* gap, Lily." You'd think she would applaud me for cultivating a successful dog-walking business and social media presence—and now spinning those off with a collection of dog crafts that people are actually buying. But Mom thinks my entrepreneurial efforts are a "distraction."

She won't let go of reminding me that getting a college degree should be my priority. "Accumulating likes and knitting sweaters for Chihuahuas won't prepare you for how to *think*, Lily."

I don't just *think* she's wrong. I *know* it.

I definitely thought I needed to see my boyfriend, sooner rather than later! Escaping my mother and what lately feels like our very, very small apartment was a bonus.

"He'll be here," I said to Mark, although I was starting to get concerned. "And please don't call me Lily Bear in a foreign country. I get to be a new person here, not the family baby." I couldn't believe I was in London! I'd never traveled so far abroad and already I was enamored. The Tube! The accents! The Cadbury chocolates! Of course, I'd experienced a lifetime of public transportation, the English language, and quality treats, but in London, they all felt exotic and new. I loved when the subway conductors told passengers getting on and off the train cars to "Mind the gap." Every time I heard the conductor's "Mind the gap" announcement, I felt like it was a secret nod to my gap year, and a secret acknowledgment that maybe London would be the place I'd figure out what I'd do once that gap period was over. Not what everyone else wanted me to do—what *I* wanted. Mind *that* gap, Mom.

The event was supposed to start at 6:00 p.m., I mean 18:00, I think? Too much math! Mark assured me that bookstore events never start on time, but the room was filled with people expecting it to start, and Dash was nowhere in sight, despite my very specific invitation in that day's Advent calendar gift from me to him. It was, simply, a note:

Daunt Books/Marylebone, 6PM, 21 December.
For the pure thrill of unreluctant desire.

How could Dash resist? He loves a treasure hunt, especially if it's a literary one. Our relationship started because of clues we left each other in a red Moleskine notebook at the Strand Bookstore during the Christmas season two years ago. This year, I decided to continue that tradition, but with a British spin. Just after Thanksgiving, I mailed Dash a handmade Advent calendar. There's little I love more than adding a new Christmas tradition, and I love the British for their Advent calendars, which begin on December 1 and end on December 24, to herald the days till Christmas. It was quite a project, as there are infinite ways to make an Advent calendar. Thanks, Pinterest—I literally lost a week of my life to researching craft ideas. But I loved the final result.

The Advent calendar I made for Dash was crafted out of a wooden book storage box. The cover opened to reveal twenty-four custom-crafted little boxes within, each having a window to open on the designated day, revealing a little gift inside. Most of these presents were of the stocking-stuffer variety, like Christmas socks, teas, and chocolates, but others were more personal, like:

December 1—a £50 gift card for Pret a Manger, Dash's

favorite English lunch haunt. He's obsessed with their cheddar and chutney sandwiches and says they're far superior to the ones Pret sells at their locations in NYC.

December 5—a ticket to see this season's Christmas blockbuster movie, *Cyborg Santa*, in 3-D. Dash's review of the movie: "Die Harder, Santa."

December 8—a gift certificate for infinite CuddleBucks. I knew he'd never redeem such a corny gift but just imagining him squirm at the sight of it gave me a good giggle.

December 14—my personal favorite, a mini-USB stick that has a photo series I personally wrangled (and by wrangled, I mean *wrangled*) of my dog, Boris, a giant bullmastiff who does not like being dressed up in Christmas decorations, dressed up in Christmas decorations and "posing" in front of some of Dash's favorite New York locations, like the Strand, the Prospect Park Bandshell, and the New York Public Library.

December 17—a Lego minifigure of Truman Capote.

Today—the invitation to Daunt Books. When I originally sent the Advent calendar with this day's gift, my intention was to beckon Dash to a London event I knew about through my cousin Mark that I thought Dash would enjoy. I hadn't known then that Dash's real gift for the day would be me showing up in person!

6:15 p.m.

Mark's new wife, Julia, joined us at the cash register station. "I think I should start soon," she said.

"Please can we wait a few more minutes?" I asked her. "I know he'll be here soon."

"Maybe there's a delay on the Tube," Julia said, trying to be kind. "I'll give it a few more minutes."

Her voice was hesitant, which I thought unusual for someone so confident. I knew she was nervous, but not because of whether or not Dash showed up. When I'd arrived at her and Mark's flat the night before, she'd gone through all the details of how this literary scavenger hunt she'd masterminded would work, and after hearing it? Yes, I'd be nervous, too.

My cousin Mark, who used to work at the Strand Bookstore in New York, took a vacation to England a year ago, and one of his destinations in London was Daunt Books, a bookstore that had been recommended to him as being particularly enchanting. For him, indeed it was. At Daunt's Marylebone location, in an Edwardian three-level store with oak balconies, blue-green walls, a conservatory ceiling, and stained-glass windows, he met Julia Gordon, a Jamaican-Jewish Londoner who had just taken a marketing job at Daunt after finishing her PhD in English literature at Cambridge. We still can't believe she got Mark to move to London or that Mark got her to marry him.

Julia dreams of starting a literary tour business, and she was looking for ways to promote the bookstore at the holidays, so she created this first-ever Daunt Books Bibliophile Cup Challenge, which Dash would learn about if he showed up when the Advent calendar told him to show. It wasn't my jet lag bewildering me about whether Julia's plan could work. I was more concerned she was one of those people who are brilliant but with no practical sense. I'm from a family of academics—I know these people. When she'd explained how the hunt would work, I could see there were details she hadn't thought through. Like, is there a foreign dignitary visiting who would cause traffic problems or massive protests? Is there a Santa convention that's going to cause foot traffic to get out of hand? Fickle customers. WEATHER. I'm a dog-walker in New York. I always have to think about these practical things. Julia lives inside books. She doesn't have to deal with reality as frequently as the rest of us. But I supported her entrepreneurial ambition and wanted to encourage it the way I wish my mom did for mine.

"Good turnout," Mark said proudly to his new wife, looking relieved. Julia had spread the word through social media, but who knew if people would really show up to chase book clues right before Christmas?

There were probably twenty people gathered in the center of the store, at the designated meeting area. Then my heart dropped. And it wasn't because Dash *wasn't* there yet. It was because of who *was* there. I spied a young couple. I wasn't sure they were indeed who I thought they were until the girl—she wore a lovely, emerald-colored silk hijab just like one I'd seen in Oxford photos Dash had sent me from university—said to the guy, "Olivier, Team Brasenose for the win, right?" And the Olivier guy smiled at her in a way Dash never smiles at me, with a fierce sense of entitlement, and said, "Azra. Darling. It's done."

Fa la la la FROCKKKKKK!!!!!!!!!

It was Olivier Wythe-Jones and Azra Khatun, two of his classmates at Oxford. He associates them with everything he dislikes about Oxford.

British universities are very different from American ones. You don't major in a subject, you "read" it. You "sit" for exams (while wearing academic robes!) rather than "take" exams. Freshmen are "freshers." You only study one subject at school and nothing else. Instead of semesters, there are three eight-week terms with funny-sounding names: Michaelmas, Hilary, and Trinity. (I know, it makes as much sense as how Brits tell time or why they refer to their money in terms of weight.) Universities are actually a collection of different colleges, each with their own unique identity, like Hogwarts houses, which is very cool of them. At Oxford, Dash applied to "read" classics and literature at Brasenose College specifically because the rooms there are singles. While he didn't get a roommate, he still shared too-close proximity with students he had no desire to befriend. The power couple of Brasenose were this Olivier Wythe-Jones and Azra Khatun duo—or, as Dash described them, "Like if Draco Malfoy was dating Fleur Delacour."

I was almost starting to hope Dash didn't show up.

But I was getting irritated as well. No one knows Dash better than me, or so I thought. He would never not accept a literary challenge. He's that much of a nerd. It's why I love him so much. And we've been together for two years. Shouldn't he, like, *sense* that I was nearby? Shouldn't he *sense* how much his beloved had sacrificed to give him this great Christmas surprise? I walked away from dog-walking at the busiest time of year! I allowed my brother to cover my job while I'm away! I gave Langston as much training as possible, but I was worried. Would I have dog-walking clients to return to when I got home to New York?

A bald man wearing a raincoat who looked well into his middle age came up to me. He said, "I hope you don't mind me asking, but could I get a picture with you?"

My overprotective cousin Mark eyed him warily. "Why do you need a picture with her?"

The man said, "You're Lily the dog-walker, right?"

I nodded. It happens sometimes now; I get recognized. Ever since that huge, dog-loving social media personality highlighted my account on Instagram, my follower numbers have exploded. Also, I was named one of the Top Ten Dog-fluencers to Watch in the latest issue of *Dog People* magazine, a copy of which the man had in his hand. I even started selling dog crafts through my site. To my surprise, people bought my products! Like, a lot of them.

Mark grudgingly took a photo of me with the man, who asked me, "Are you in town for the Canine Supporters World Education Conference?"

"I wish," I said. My ticket home was for very early the morning of December 26. Even if the week before Christmas was one of my busiest workweeks, I could still eke out escaping to London for it. But the week *between* Christmas and New

Year's is the highest of high seasons for dog-walkers. I couldn't be away for that, which was when the GOADC (Greatest of All Dog Conferences) in London was taking place.

It was all I could do not to blurt out what I hadn't even yet told Dash, or my parents. The organization that sponsored the conference, Pembroke Canine Facilitator Institute (PCFI), was the very learning institution that had offered me admission for next term! PCFI is like the Harvard of dog education schools, and if I hadn't told anyone yet, it was because I wanted to see how I'd like London first—and also my parents will kill me. They were super not into me deferring Barnard for a year and they will see the PCFI program as me trying to stall college, if not outright kill that prospect.

They'd be right.

6:20 p.m.

"I need to start, Lily," said Julia. "Sorry."

Where *was* he? "I understand," I said, frustrated. I'd put so much expectation into this moment of Dash discovering me here at this event. And he hadn't bothered to show. I was determined not to ruin the moment of surprise by texting him: *Where ARE you?*

Julia spoke into a microphone to the gathered crowd. "Thank you for coming, everybody! I'm Julia Gordon, the marketing manager here at Daunt, and this is our first-ever, hopefully annual, Daunt Books Bibliophile Cup Challenge!"

No one said anything. "Why aren't people cheering?" I whispered to Mark.

"British people don't cheer. That's so American."

"But what about soccer?"

"Okay, they cheer then. But there's usually a lot of beer first."

Julia continued, holding up an iPad. "I have your team names collected here. When your team name is called, please send a representative up for your first clue. You'll get points for finding each destination, with bonus points awarded to members who answer trivia questions at each spot. Once you complete each clue, another one will be emailed to your team leader. The last clues will be emailed the morning of the twenty-third. I'll be tallying your scores here on my iPad based on my team members' evaluations at each destination. On Christmas Eve, the two highest-scoring teams will receive Daunt gift cards commensurate with their tallied points. Good luck, everyone! And thank you for participating."

Mark called out, "And that other thing!"

Julia sighed ever so slightly. "Yes. My American husband insists there must be an actual *prize* for people to show off, so . . ."

Mark pulled something from beneath a table of mystery books and brought it to where Julia was addressing the crowd. It was a giant trophy, taller than my very large dog, shaped like a stack of books instead of a more typical trophy cup. "The Daunt Books Bibliophile Cup!" said Mark, to no one's applause.

Mentally, I was cheering Mark on, like, *Yes, a trophy!* But I could see the British crowd was unimpressed. Or if they were impressed, they bloody well weren't going to show it.

Julia handed out envelopes with the first clues to each team as Mark returned to where I was standing, holding the envelope meant for me and Dash. We were supposed to be Team Strand. "Guess it's going to be you and me on this hunt, kid," Mark said.

He opened the envelope and we read the first clue:

Near the heath
Where the bathers find their ponds
Here lies one whose name was writ in water.

"Too easy," said Mark.

"You're right," I said. I didn't think the clue was easy at all; I had no idea what it meant. I meant Mark had been right about Dash. "I shouldn't have tried to surprise him."

I love my cousin. But I traveled all this way for a treasure hunt with my boyfriend, not Mark.

I'd waited so long. I wanted to see Dash's scruffy hair and beard. His scowl. His skinny black jeans and whatever excellent sweater he favored at the moment. I assured myself, *Christmas is not ruined. It's no big deal. I'll find Dash and it's all a big mistake and—*

Suddenly the front door of the store swung open and in walked an older lady wearing a fancy suit, walking a cat on a leash. Ugh. Cat people. "Are we late?" she asked loudly in a regal British accent, but like the kind that possibly could be a fake accent adopted by someone who is really from Sheepshead Bay, Brooklyn. A gentleman dressed in an elegant suit with a top hat followed behind her. He took off his hat with a flourish and tipped it in her direction. "Never, my dear," he told her. "The world waits for you."

The gentleman was Dash. DASH! My sweetheart! His long hair was gone, and his face was clean-shaven. Looking cheerful. *Smiling.*

And suddenly I realized: That person I thought I knew best? I didn't know him at all.

two

DASH

December 21st

This is the story of a boy who lost something, then found something, then had to figure out what to do next.

It starts off, strangely enough, with a sweatshirt, child's-size medium.

I was seven, maybe eight. I got home from school, went to the kitchen for a snack, and found a box waiting on the kitchen table, covered in stamps that featured a woman I vaguely recognized as a queen. Even though she'd been post-marked and run a little ragged from the journey, her regal countenance didn't waver. I admired that, and studied the package further, realizing with a shock and a thrill that my name was on it, which meant that it was for me.

"It's from your grandmother," my mother said when she caught me examining it. She said this with much more shock than thrill.

Immediately my young mind sizzled a connection, and for at least a few years after that, my mental image of my grandmother matched the face on the stamp. This was my father's mother, a woman I couldn't remember meeting in person. The things my parents said about her were not things I could fathom, starting with the fact that she'd left my grandfather because she'd fallen in love with a stone. I heard my mother explain this to her friends when my father wasn't around; my grandmother had landed in England because she'd fallen in love with a stone. She hadn't ended up with this stone (this made more sense to me), but it had been the reason for her to move to London, to start what my mother called "a new life." People always asked my mother *which stone,* and she said she wasn't sure, that this had happened long before she came into the picture. It was only when I overheard one of these conversations later in life, in my early teens, that I understood what had happened. It wasn't a stone she was chasing, but a member of the Rolling Stones.

She called every year for my father's birthday. He answered dutifully, not enthusiastically. The phone would get passed to my mother, then to me. My grandmother always seemed delighted to talk to me, but I never knew what to say.

She had sent toys and stuffed animals when I'd been born, and later I would uncover a photo of her holding my bundled baby body in her arms. This photo was not on display in our apartment; I had to dig into a baby book to find it, just like I had to dig into my parents' wedding album to find another photo of her, beaming in a pink paisley dress as she gave my father away. (My grandfather and his new wife had skipped the wedding because of extensive golfing plans and a vague distrust of my father's ability to choose wisely.)

I'd never received a package from her before, and its timing (nowhere near my birthday) made it extra tantalizing. She'd been overly generous with the packing tape, so there was no way for me to open the box without the intervention of my mother's knife. The fact that the package had traveled over an ocean made it seem even more magical, and its contents did not disappoint—which means, I suppose, that they *appointed*. There were Cadbury chocolates, the likes of which I'd never experienced before. There were paperback editions of Roald Dahl with covers entirely unlike the American ones. There was a toy truck whose name I believed to be Laurie until my mother explained it was spelled a different way. Wrapped in the arts section from the Sunday *Guardian*, there was a piece of red felt that was revealed to be the northernmost tip of Paddington Bear. And then, at the bottom of the box, there was a sweatshirt with the Oxford University crest. I put it on immediately, and it fit perfectly.

Pinned to the sweatshirt was a short note.

> *I thought you might like these.*
> *Consider it a gift for no reason.*
> *Love, Grandmum*

I was enchanted.

My father, when he came home, was more acerbic. "Are

you kidding me?" was his reaction when told about the package.

My mother insisted that I write a thank-you note, and I mustered up my finest penmanship to do so. Thus began a pattern that lasted for more than a decade: Out of the blue, my grandmother would send me a package, always with Cadbury chocolates and always with books, and I would reply with a thank-you note that gave her the slimmest of glimpses into my life alongside much more voluminous reactions to the books she had sent. This was how we corresponded. The relationship didn't require much more than that, which suited both of us well.

In the meantime, my fantasy of Oxford set in. It was my literary utopia, a beacon of erudition in a world that seemed to increasingly despise the learned. Anytime a classmate disdained me or derided me, I imagined there were plenty of people at Oxford who would understand exactly what I meant. Every time my father or mother looked at me as if to say *How did our merged DNA conjure this pedantic cypher?*, I would picture a kind Oxford professor who would admire my inquisitiveness rather than be mystified by it or feel betrayed by it.

The downside of knowing this better place existed was the nagging, constant doubt that I would ever be good enough to be admitted through its gates. What if what I intended as profound insight was revealed to be mere bloviation? What if I read all the right books and surveyed all the right thinkers but couldn't manage to string together the right words myself? There's a thin, unpredictable line between *aspirant* and *pretender*, and it shifted so often in my mind that I never knew where I stood. As the application process began, it felt like the worst kind of reckoning—I could endure my schoolmates calling me pretentious or weird if my own idiosyncratic self-education came to be respected by the people I actually respected. But if Oxford said I didn't pass muster? It would be devastating—and that was exactly what I was expecting in my dark, insecure heart.

Then, much to my surprise, they let me in.

My mother was with me when I found out, and she and I hugged and cried and felt as close as we'd ever been. Hours later, it hit her how far away I was going to be, which tinged her excitement with a certain *eau d'empty nest*. I waited two days to tell my father and only did so because there was no way of getting around it. He had his own life now, away from my mother and mostly away from me. I interrupted from time to time, to witness his foolhardy attempts at fatherishness. When I told him I'd been admitted to Oxford, he congratulated me—not with a hug, but with that simple word, *congratulations*. Then, almost in the same breath, he asked me how much it was going to cost. When I told him, he murmured something noncommittal, then asked me where else I'd applied. I'd given him the full list the previous time we'd dined, but I repeated it again, making the other options as lifeless as possible so my position would be clear.

Luckily for me, my father's friends must have been impressed when he told them his son had gotten into Oxford;

whereas I imagined a bastion of poets wrestling with their own despondency as a way of pulling the world out of its mire, my father and his friends saw a breeding ground for Future Leaders. Understanding the entitled direction that wind was blowing, I made my prime ministrations to my father along Future Leader lines, and after some cutthroat negotiations that got far more personal than they objectively needed to be, my parents worked out the tuition question.

It was only then, when I knew the dream was in fact coming true, that I told Lily. We had been assuming we'd both be staying in the New York area—she'd been admitted to Barnard and I'd been admitted to Columbia. Now I was mucking that up, and wanted to be sure I wasn't mucking up our future as well.

I took her to Elephant & Castle to break the news over scones and tea. Perhaps because I had chosen a British-themed establishment for the delivery scene, she didn't seem particularly surprised. It was incredible, really: She knew how much Oxford meant to me, and was thrilled on my behalf in a way that nobody else in my life had managed to muster.

"But what about us being together in the city?" I asked.

"We can work it out," she promised. And I believed her in a way I'd never believe in myself. Because Lily always keeps her promises, even if she has to shoulder the world and bend time in order to do so.

We knew long distance would be hard, especially considering my disinclination toward the digital tether. I didn't want to rely on texting and FaceTiming and writing witty, sweet comments under each other's posts as a way of keeping the kindling under our love.

"My favorite things about you are in-person things," I told Lily, and it was true. I promised to write her letters and to figure out a way for us to travel to Europe together before she started Barnard and I started my second year. I wasn't going to be tempted to play the field or sow my oats; for me, Lily was the field, and she could have all of my oats. She didn't fit perfectly into my new life, but the beauty of our relationship is that she hadn't fit perfectly into my old life, either. Love teaches you that fitting is overrated; what you need to do is change the shape of your life to make the connection. We'd done it before; we'd do it again.

It was hard at first. I'd sit in my room and listen to Death Cab for Cutie's "Transatlanticism" (the song, not the album) on repeat.

I need you so much closer . . .

I'd write her letters on the backs of Oxford postcards.

I need you so much closer . . .

I'd call her to hear her voice, to hear what she had to say, to experience the reassurance of her hearing me.

This was during the first two weeks of school. Then, fiercely and relentlessly, Oxford took over my life.

The scenes on those postcards were the scenes I'd carried in my head ever since the sweatshirt had caused my curiosity to bloom. Verdant lawns and sophisticated cathedrals of learning. Gargoyle guardians keeping watch beneath cornices. Iron gates older than most of the books we'd read.

Blackwell's bookstore and the Bodleian Library, opening their shelves to the whims of genius and the genius of whims. The hallowed ground felt wide open, the citadel of knowledge entered at last. That was my postcard version.

The problem was that the postcards tended to show empty lawns, empty buildings. I hadn't taken into account that there would be other people walking on these paths, crowding these gateways, pulling books from the shelves, talking loudly into their phones, and texting laboriously as if their minds and communication skills had been fully outsourced to Apple.

I had thought Oxford students would be more sophisticated, more intellectually grounded, more literarily impassioned than anyone else.

But it ended up that they were teenagers just like everyone else.

I hadn't escaped the world after all. Instead, the world had infiltrated my ideal. I found some friends—kind and generous and bookish friends, for sure. But we were surrounded by petty, cliquish, self-entitled, self-branding, status-obsessed, neurotic, insecure, egomaniacal, interpersonally political, emotionally haphazard, academically specious, conversationally tedious humblebraggarts as well.

In other words, I had gotten to my dream place, and it only left me glum.

The university made rigorous demands, and I liked to think I was up to the tasks. I reveled in a poetry class I was taking and tried to muster my way elsewhere. When I got out of class, I wanted to go back to my dorm room to read; I would have been happy to spend the whole night reading. But my next-door neighbor, a future cabinet minister named John, was dedicated to inviting people over for lager and pontification. I played along, didn't want to be the kill-joy even if it meant sacrificing my own joy on the altar of alcohol and keeping face.

I started to sleep later and later, as if my body was willing itself back to New York time. I was honest with Lily about how hard it was, but I also made sure to tell my surroundings to her as if they were an interesting story, with compelling characters and narrative thrust. The fact that I myself didn't feel this thrust? I tried to chalk it up to first-year jitters, even if that chalk was easily washed away under the sponge of any scrutiny.

I wasn't rising to the heights I had expected. Nobody else around me seemed to be doing so, either—but for whatever reason, they didn't seem to care.

I had sent my grandmother a rare non-thank-you note when I'd solidified my Oxford plans, to let her know we'd soon be sharing a country code. She'd called immediately after receiving the note, telling me I had to drop by her flat in Waterloo whenever I wanted.

"Consider it your home away from your home away from home," she said in an accent that was mostly posh, but with traces of American charm underneath.

I'd thought I'd wait for a break to head Londonward, but

after three weeks of Oxford, I phoned her and said I needed a brief escape; she told me she needed a little more warning for Saturday night plans, but that her Sunday was entirely free. I took the bus into "town" and made my way to Roupell Street, a short walk from Waterloo Station along the South Bank. It was my first time in the city, and I got turned around repeatedly. Without my phone's guidance, I probably would have ended up in the Thames. I was fifteen minutes late, but when my grandmother answered her red door on her quiet lane, she didn't seem perturbed.

In person, she was not at all like the stamp version of the Queen. If anything, she looked like another kind of Queen, the type that could get into a rhapsodic tizzy over being bohemian. Her hair was a stylish shag, her clothes still in the same bright vocabulary as the pink paisley she'd worn to my parents' wedding. The most striking thing, though, was how much she looked like me. We actually appeared more like each other than either of us appeared like my father. It was uncanny.

"Oh, wow," she said after opening the door. "Would you look at that?"

Speakers throughout the flat were releasing the sound of George Harrison into every room. She bade me put down my bag in the hallway and immediately launched into a tour of the two floors, highlighting the guest room as mine for the duration of my time in the United Kingdom. Where I would have had shelves of books, she had shelves of vinyl.

Her décor was very mod—she even had a chair that dropped from the ceiling in its own orb, hovering beside a lime-green couch.

Instead of sitting in the sitting room, she took me to the kitchen, where a late breakfast awaited us on an old wood table. As we sipped tea (hers "flavored" with a "dab" of whisky) and ate pastries, we caught up on the past nineteen years of my life without mentioning my parents in anything other than passing. When I felt I was talking too much about myself, I'd steer the conversation her way; she'd dole out a fact or two (she worked in the arts; she wasn't seeing anyone in particular at the moment but had a few suitors), and then she'd steer the conversation back to me. I told her what I really thought about Oxford, and she didn't scold me for ingratitude or tell me to get over myself. Instead she said, "Well, Oxford can only give you one part of your education; we'll have to work on the rest."

We stayed talking in her kitchen for hours. She told me she liked Lily, from the sound of her. And she told me she didn't like my neighbor John, from the sound of him. Then, lastly, when we came to a natural pause, she told me, "I have to say, I like you very much, Dash. I'm so glad our paths have unfolded in this way."

I felt glad; I felt grateful.

I returned to Oxford with an open invitation to London, and as the weeks passed and the walls of my dorm room seemed to close in on me more and more, I took my grandmother up on it frequently. She introduced me to her friends and took me to art exhibits, concerts at the Royal Albert, and theater on the West End. She told me to call her Gem, like her friends did; since I'd never really called her Grand-mum out loud, it was an easy enough transition to make. When we met her friends or acquaintances, she always in-troduced me as her grandson, which didn't particularly take my notice until Carl, one of her painter friends, said, "You have to understand how much that means; it's the closest to acknowledging her age that I've ever seen Gem go."

Gem and I never talked about my father, and I certainly never told him that I was seeing so much of his mother. When my own mother came to visit over Thanksgiving (since she had a break and I didn't), I debated whether or not to take her to London. But Gem insisted ("I always liked your mother, even if I questioned her taste in men," she quipped), and miraculously, Gem won over my mother as well. Before Thanksgiving, when Gem had told me, "You simply *must* stay for Christmas," I had thought, *Yes, I simply must*. Now my mother, who often went away for the holidays herself, understood my reasoning.

Lily didn't take it as well. I called her, because I knew it would be something that required conversation, not the noël cowardice of a text or email. She didn't try to hide her disap-pointment, and I appreciated that—we were still being en-tirely honest with each other, and all the long-distance trust was built on that. I offered to fly her over, but she said she needed to be with her family, and I couldn't argue with that.

I missed her so much. The fact that I was staying for

Christmas didn't contradict that. I told her this, and told her I just needed to get my footing here. Oxford was battering my soul to a pulp, and London was the only balm I had for that. New York would have brought me Lily, but it also would have brought me a hundred other obligations. She said she understood.

A few days later, a homemade Advent calendar arrived in the mail. Her way of being here, and of helping me through.

Hallmate John and his Oxford cohort—led by Azra, Queen of Snide; Olivier, King of Glide—thought the Advent calendar was "cute" . . . an adjective I sensed they usually reserved for animals that fit into a teacup. This cohort partied far harder than it studied, and they managed to be impressing the tutors far more than I was.

I refused to let them make me feel bad about Lily's creation (though I did hide the gift certificate for cuddling far, far in the back of my sock drawer). I remembered that first box that Gem had sent me and decided to re-create it for Lily. I bought Cadbury chocolates, a toy lorry, some childhood-favorite tomes in their British dressings, and an Oxford sweatshirt. Not a gift for no reason but a gift for reason. I wrapped it in brown paper, tied it in string, and sent it across the ocean.

Then I stared down the hardest exams I'd ever faced. And instead of staring them into submission, I blinked. And blinked. And blinked some more. By the end of it, I felt like I was all eyelid and no pupil. And I must have looked gutted as well, because when I showed up on Gem's doorstep immediately after my final exam, she took one look at me and said, "Oh, dear."

"I think I need to sleep for a few weeks," I told her. "Can you wake me up when it's midnight on New Year's, and then let me go back to sleep?"

"You have four hours to nap," she replied, "and then I'll wake you up with a plan."

Precisely four hours later, there was a knock on my door. I was still too sleepy to know whether I called out "Come in" or just thought about doing so. Either way, she came in.

She said, "I've looked into my crystal ball" (this is what she called her smartphone), "and I believe I've found an event that will put the bubbles back in your champagne."

"Does it involve other people?" I grumbled.

"Certainly."

"Nooooooo," I replied, mostly to the pillow I was pulling over my face.

"Dash," my grandmother said in her most leveling voice, "you must come to grips with the fact that you'd make a very inept monk. Tonight you get to be the dandy and I get to be the wayward contessa. And instead of teaming up to solve country-house crimes, we'll go on a literary escapade. If that's not a tonic for your ills, I don't know what is."

Even in my world-weary, sleep-deprived state, I had to admit that, put in those terms, it sounded like a pretty good plan.

"You sound like Mrs. Basil E.," I mumbled, referring to Lily's great-aunt, who also liked a proper turn of phrase.

"Groovy," Gem said, dispelling any aura of Mrs. Basil E. that might have gathered, since I doubted highly that Mrs. Basil E. would have used that word even at the height of its innovation. "Now let's get going."

I groaned my agreement and peeked out from under the pillow to see my grandmother gripped by a fervor she usually saved for her love of Eric Clapton and David Thewlis and her loathing of Damien Hirst and the Tories.

"Lovely!" she chirped. "I'll gather the *accoutrements*."

Soon the *Red Hot + Blue* album—a favorite of hers—filled the air. I got out of bed and walked over to Lily's Advent calendar, which had been the first thing I'd unpacked before my nap collapse. I looked at the doorway that led to today's gift and felt I didn't yet deserve to open it; this was the drawback of an Advent calendar, because I felt that I actually needed to have done something on that day to be worthy of whatever small piece of affection Lily had packed inside. I figured I still had a few hours left and could open it when I got home.

Next I went into the bathroom and made the grave mistake of (a) turning on the light and (b) looking in the mirror. I knew, intellectually, that my aversion to finding an Oxford barber and my inability to find time for a haircut had led to a certain follicular expansiveness. But now I realized that I had veered from Bright Young Thing territory straight into the land of Robinson Crusoe.

"It's time for a lather and a shave!" I called out to Gem.

"And how about a snip and a style when you're through?"

she called back. (This was how I found out she'd worked for three years as a hairdresser at a posh salon.)

Two hours later, I bore a better resemblance to an older me, the one my university self had bamboozled, bedraggled, and balderdashed. Gem's wardrobe included a few upscale suits that fit me beautifully. (This was how I found out she'd worked as a consultant to Liberty for two years.) She even had a top hat on reserve, left behind by a not-quite-gentleman who'd left her behind as well.

I went into my room and put on my duds; when I emerged, I found Gem in a similar suit of a much more flamboyant color.

"Aren't we just the pair?" she said with a smile.

"Swellegant, for sure," I parlayed.

If school had become a dirge, this was a blast of sonata. I half expected a carriage to be waiting for us when Gem opened the front door. But instead we rode on the Tube, reveling in the bemused looks we got from The General Population. I took a picture of us to send to Lily but didn't have reception underground. I imagined Gem pulling out a third suit for Lily to wear and the three of us taking the town together. It could happen.

We got off at Marylebone and paraded to Daunt Books. I had spent a good amount of time at Waterstones Piccadilly, which looked like a flagship that had sailed in from the Jazz Age. Daunt, meanwhile, looked like a place where Jane Austen and Charles Dickens would have hung out to thumb-wrestle or brood on the state of the novel, such as it was.

"Who's reading tonight?" I asked as we approached, still in the dark.

"Not a reading. Something else," Gem replied. Then: "Oh, look at that."

A few steps away from us, a cat was walking without an owner attached to its leash.

As Gem stooped over to check the cat for a tag, I asked, "Is that a British thing, to keep a cat on a leash?"

"No more or no less than anywhere else." Gem shook her head. "No identification. So careless. Perhaps she belongs to someone inside—it's cruel to keep her out here, so let's take her in."

As we walked into the store, we saw that we were catching the evening's activity in medias res. All eyes turned our way—perhaps because of the cat?—and Gem made the most of the moment, drolly asking, "Are we late?" To which I replied, "Never, my dear. The world waits for you."

After the dread of exam season, the dark cloud of wondering if I really belonged at Oxford, I felt such delight in the dialogue, delirium in our flight of fancy. I still had no idea what we were doing here, but I instinctively knew that whatever it was would be far better than a night of stress and sensibility in my dorm room. I honestly didn't think things could get any better—and then I scanned the crowd and saw Lily's face looking back at me.

At first I thought: *This can't be possible. I must still be napping.*

Then I thought: *This must be Gem's surprise. She is a magician.*

If it wasn't a dream, it must have been planned. But if it had been planned, why did Lily look so confused?

I headed straight to her and wrapped her in an embrace.

"I can't believe it!" I said. "You're here!"

"I'm here," she said, hugging me back, sounding (yes) a little confused. Then, when we pulled apart a little, she added, "I thought you had a beard? And long hair?"

Gem's voice came from over my shoulder. "A momentary lapse that shan't be repeated."

I smiled at her. "How did you do this? How did you get Lily here without telling me?"

Gem's eyes grew wider. "This is Lily?! Well, that explains a lot."

"I got here myself," Lily said. "Who's this?"

"This is my grandmother!" I told her. "Gem, meet Lily. Lily, meet Gem. This is too amazing—two of my favorite people in the world in one place!"

Neither of their smiles seemed to match my own.

I felt something startling against my leg, then realized it was just the cat.

"Is she yours?" Lily asked.

"Just a foundling," I said. "We should probably see if anyone here claims her as their own."

But nobody made any move to take the leash. The mood had quickly shifted from curiosity to impatience. Another familiar face came into view—that of Lily's disputatious cousin Mark. I'd forgotten he'd moved to London.

"He isn't going to be on our team, is he?" Mark asked, cordial as ever.

"We'd love to be on your team, Lily," Gem said, swatting at Mark's gnat-like words.

"Oh," Lily said.

I reached out and took her hand.

But still, it took a few seconds for her to reach her decision.

three

LiLY

December 21st

I wanted Dash to be on my team, of course. That's why I came to London.

But this Gem person?

Not so sure.

I should have been happy for Dash that he finally had a family member he genuinely liked, not just someone he loved (Mom) or tolerated (Dad) out of obligation. But it required a complete shift in my perspective of Dash to see him getting on so well with his grandmother. Dash is someone who avoids family members. That's who he is. It's how I understand him. That's why he evolved into such a book person from childhood. Books were his escape from them.

"You look very fancy," I told Dash, admiring his posh clothes and clean-shaven face, while also missing his now-shorn scruff.

He tipped his hat to me. "Thank you."

Gem put her arm around me like we'd known each other for years, not minutes. "You are an impossible sausage of adorable," she pronounced.

I wouldn't . . . I wouldn't . . . I wouldn't . . . I couldn't help it! I was immediately falling into potential deep dislike of Dash's beloved grandmother. Who doesn't like a senior lady who used to be a very cool groupie who now carted her grandson to literary challenges? Who is that evil and unkind? Possibly me.

Also, who brings a cat on a leash into a bookstore?

"There you are, Moriarty!" said Julia, who had found her way over to our group. She picked up the cat, who swatted Julia's face in protest but then nestled his head into the crook of her neck with great affection, a very feline game of love me/love me not. "He belongs to the bookstore owner. I left him in the office an hour ago. I don't know how he got out."

"Open window?" I suggested.

"Probably," she said, unconcerned that her error could have caused CAT-astrophic consequences for Moriarty if he'd slipped out the window and then gotten hit by a car.

"Why does he have a leash?" I asked.

"A leash?" Julia looked confused.

"A lead," Mark said. "That's what they call a leash here."

Calling a leash a "lead"? Now *that* was an impossible sausage of adorable.

"I guess I left his lead on after taking him for his walk," Julia said, again unconcerned by the inconvenience she'd caused to the cat, both left to fend for himself on the streets of London, and with an unattended leash attached to his neck that could cause any number of problems. Humans. I don't understand them. So many of them don't think things through when it comes to our fur friends.

"Is he the house cat here at the bookstore?" Gem asked, leaning in for a pet on Moriarty, which was greeted by another swat. I was starting to really like this Moriarty.

"Our best employee," said Julia. "Keeps the rodents at bay and keeps the boss calm."

Mark said, "Are we ready to hit the streets, Team Strand?"

I wasn't ready, especially not after Gem said, "I was so excited when I read about this literary challenge. I knew it was exactly what Dash would love to do."

Wait. Gem thought bringing Dash here was *her* idea?

"Did you open today's Advent calendar box?" I asked Dash.

"Not yet," he said cheerfully.

That was the box that contained the message directing him here. So he was here because Gem brought him, not me. He didn't seem concerned at all that he'd neglected my day's Advent gift to him.

I wouldn't . . . I wouldn't . . . I couldn't help it. I was jealous and enraged. I traveled thousands of miles across an ocean and left my dog-walking business in the care of my brother, who doesn't even like dogs that much, so I could take Dash on this literary adventure. Not so Gem could think it was *her* idea!

I imagined biting into a delightful piece of chocolate cake baked by British grande dame baker Mary Berry herself to avoid a sourpuss expression appearing on my face. Dash looked so *happy*. I didn't want to ruin it.

I didn't have to. The couple I'd been worried about Dash noticing now made themselves noticeable, coming over to greet our group.

"Dash, old fellow! You look inappropriately dapper," said Dash's classmate. I remembered how Dash had told me he cringed every time Olivier called him "old fellow," because he suspected Olivier said it only so he would sound like the aristocratic British prick stereotype he expected Americans wanted to hear.

Dash didn't exactly frown, but his eyebrows furrowed, in a way I knew to express displeasure, as if someone served him green tea when he is strictly a black-tea-only old fellow.

"Hello, Olivier," said Dash. "Hello, Azra." His voice sounded a bit dead. He gestured to me and then to Gem. "This is my girlfriend, Lily. And my grandmother Gem."

"And I'm Lily's cousin Mark," my cousin Mark added. "I'm Dash's favorite of Lily's relatives."

He's not, of course. Insulting or annoying Dash is usually my brother's favored sport, but when he's not available, Mark is always keen to step in. I'd feel bad for Dash except I think he expects them to give him a hard time and would be disappointed if they didn't. Langston and Mark are like the brothers Dash never had and never wanted. It's a relationship that works for them, so I stay out of it.

Dash ignored Mark and told Gem, "Olivier and Azra are my classmates at Brasenose."

"Marvelous!" said Gem. "Are you playing the Daunt Books Bibliophile Cup Challenge also?"

"We are," said Azra.

"And we intend to win," said Olivier.

"How predictably overcompetitive of you, Olivier," said Dash.

"I had no idea a bibliophile challenge could be so fraught with tension," said Mark. He nodded to Olivier and Azra. "Team Strand will crush you, of course."

"Team Brasenose is not concerned," said Olivier.

I could feel Azra staring at me. She was so effortlessly chic and smart-looking that I felt intimidated, like I wanted Team Brasenose to win because she was so innately cooler than me, and I had no idea why. Finally, she said, "Are you . . . Lily Dogcrafts?"

"Yes!" I said, too eager to impress her.

Azra said, "My little sister is obsessed with your dog crafts page. She's not going to believe I've met you. Might I snap a selfie of us?"

"Sure!" I said.

As she snapped our photo, she said, "I bought her the Lily Dogcrafts raincoat for her birthday. It was at the top of her wish list."

"The raincoat with the interior lining of pockets for treats and poo bags?" It cost twenty dollars more than the regular raincoat but was a worthwhile investment, in my opinion.

"Indeed," said Azra. "In pink."

"That's the best of all the colors! I personally chose the fabric from a wholesaler that specializes in textiles for rainwear. They customized the pink option to my exact specification. I'm really proud of it."

"My sister loved it," said Azra. She turned to Dash, looking at him with what I thought might be a newfound respect. "Why didn't you tell me your girlfriend was famous?"

Olivier said, "To be honest, we didn't really believe Dash had a girlfriend back in New York."

Mark said, "To be honest, that's what her family back in New York would also like to believe."

Finally, Dash laughed, at ease. Being insulted by Mark or my brother probably feels like home to him. But it was more than that. To see Dash in a bookstore is to see Dash in the most content version of himself. Even being playfully insulted.

I wrapped my arms around Dash, both protective and proud of him. "My family adores you," I assured him.

Dash said, "Your family is so big that even if only ten percent of them like me, that's more people who like me than in my own family."

"I'm a family member that's rather fond of you," said Gem to Dash.

"That's why you're the one that matters," Dash told her.

"Americans," said Olivier contemptuously.

"I have no great affection for Dash," Mark assured Olivier.

Suddenly Moriarty leapt out of Julia's arms and sprinted toward the bookstore's front door. Immediately I sprang into action, practically mowing down several bookstore browsers as I sped after the cat. Dash knows how to handle bookstores and my relatives. I know how to handle animals taking unauthorized expeditions. Just as Moriarty was about to glide out of the open front door, I whooshed down to pick him up.

"I respect you for trying," I told Moriarty. He tried to wiggle out of my arms, but no such luck. I make a living out of these situations. I kicked the door shut and said to Julia, "Shall we return Moriarty to the safety of the office? Without his leash on? I mean, his lead?" I didn't want to scold Julia, but I couldn't help but tell her, "If you're not walking him on the lead, the lead really should be taken off, so it doesn't get caught on something that could hurt him."

"Of course," Julia said, not interested at all in my wisdom. She took Moriarty from my arms. "I'll return him to the office now. Team Strand and Team Brasenose—get to work!"

She left with the cat. Gem said to me, "I don't think she needs pet advice, my dear. If the cat wants to wander, let him!"

Grrrr.

Dash knows how little I like having my pet care advice challenged, so before I could give Gem a piece of my mind—and some badly needed animal education—he diverted the conversation. "Our first clue! Any ideas?" He read the clue aloud.

Near the heath
Where the bathers find their ponds
Here lies one whose name was writ in water.

Mark had said it was too easy, so I turned to him to decipher the clue, but he shook his head. "I have insider information on this one. I'm going to have to insist that Master Brasenose give it a go. Don't cheat by using your phone."

Dash said, "Don't have to, Master Took-Six-Years-to-Finish-His-Undergraduate-Degree. *Here lies one whose name was writ in water.* It's what Keats asked to have carved on his gravestone. As last words go . . . rather epic."

"Aren't you a genius, Dash!" said Gem. A customer passed by her carrying a stack of books toward the cash register. "He goes to Oxford," she told the uninterested customer. Then she mused aloud. "Keats . . . Keats . . . heath . . . bathers . . . ponds." She paused a moment, then: "I've got it! The first clue is probably for the Keats House museum, near the Hampstead Heath bathing ponds!"

"*You* are the genius," Dash told her.

"And there's a marvelous Indian restaurant just around the corner from the museum. I've been craving a good dosa. You?" said Gem.

"You're even *more* of a genius," Dash said to Gem.

I'd pretty much lost my appetite. I hate Indian food. At least, today I did.

Before we could exit the store, Olivier and Azra breezed past us toward the front door. As Olivier opened the door to leave, he called to Dash. "We'll wave to you from the winner's circle, old fellow."

Dash waved his two middle fingers to Olivier, who laughed and then left.

"Tube or taxi?" Mark asked Team Strand.

"Tube," Dash said.

"Taxi it is," said Mark.

We stepped outside. It had started raining but Mark was able to flag down a taxi quickly. My first London taxi! I loved the expanse of the backseat, which sat two rows of passengers facing each other. Mark and I sat next to each other, with Dash and Gem opposite us.

"Where to?" the driver asked. He had a Cockney accent straight out of *Mary Poppins*. I was so excited.

Mark gave him the address. Then I added, "Pip pip, guvnah," in my best *Mary Poppins* imitation accent.

Gem said, "They hate that here, darling Lily. Don't do an accent."

I felt my face redden, humiliated. I hadn't meant to offend.

I hadn't meant to really not like Gem, but I did. Who was she to scold my tourist enthusiasm?

Mark unzipped his briefcase. "Julia assigned these to the team captains to hand out." He took out Daunt notebooks and pens. "We're to write our letters to Father Christmas."

"To be burned up in the chimney?" Gem asked. "One of my favorite British traditions."

I'd have liked to burn up all her ideas in a chimney.

There probably wouldn't be any presents for me under the tree this year. I was a naughty, naughty girl, resentful of her boyfriend's grandmother. Seriously regretting the airfare I'd spent to come here. I didn't deserve presents.

"I don't write letters to Santa," said Dash.

Mark tossed a notebook to Dash. "Now you do."

four

DASH

December 21st

I threw the notebook right back at Mark's face and said, "No. I don't."

It was an abrupt response, and it caught all of us by surprise, myself included. I hadn't even thought about it. I'd just done it.

My body was telling me something, and I was listening to at least a part of it.

You don't have to write anything to Father Christmas, it said. Fair enough. Throw back the pad.

You don't want to be here. You have to get out of here right now. Wait a sec—what?

Don't you feel the walls of this cab getting tighter? Isn't it making your head pound? Why are you sweating so much, Dash? Don't you think you need to get out of here right this minute?

It was like exams all over again. It felt like *exams*.

And I was failing.

I was failing because I didn't want to be here in this car.

I was failing because I couldn't stand Mark. Because he was, at heart, a jerk.

I was failing because Lily was here in London and I was sure I wasn't responding the way she wanted me to.

I was failing because I had never seen her Instagram. Not once.

I was failing because I had no idea she was selling raincoats. Or was a darling of social media, if Azra's reaction was any indication.

I was failing because I thought . . . she walked dogs. I hadn't known she walked dogs so strangers would see her walk dogs and talk about her walking dogs and buy products related to her walking dogs.

I was failing because Azra and Olivier intimidated me, and that filled me with such resentment that it crowded out everything else when they were around.

I was failing because a reckoning with Keats should have been exciting me, but in truth, thinking about Keats depressed me greatly.

I was failing because I couldn't say any of these things out loud.

You're the cat on a leash, my body said. And to prove its point, it made my collar tighter and tighter.

I moved to loosen my tie, unbutton my collar.

"What's your problem?" Mark said, which was like being called a Grinch by Oscar the Grouch.

"Are you okay?" Gem asked, concern on her face.

And Lily—Lily looked confused again.

Another fail, Dash. You shouldn't be here.

"I'm sorry," I said. Which, after the fact, I understood was a strange answer to the question "Are you okay?"

"Dash?" Lily asked.

"You cold back there?" the taxi driver called to us. "Here, I'll give you more heat."

This was the last thing I wanted. Suddenly it felt like we were caught in a cashmere cloud. I sweated some more. My underarms were becoming a lake district.

Gem started to ask Lily all of the questions I should have been asking—when had she gotten in? How had the flight been? How long was she staying? I registered the answers, but not as much as I was registering the sweat, the heat, the pressure on my head, the accelerated beat of my heart. Or maybe my heartbeat was fine. I tried to take my own pulse. Ridiculous.

The taxi arrived at Keats House, just off Hampstead Heath. I leapt for the door, and only when I'd pushed outside did I realize I'd left my grandmother to pay the fare. Not particularly gallant of me.

A white shape in a black night, the Keats museum seemed almost like the ghost of a house, lit by spirits within. I hadn't expected it to be open so late, but strings must have been pulled, because I could see Azra and Olivier's team already in the entrance hall ahead of us.

"Dash?"

It was Lily again, at my elbow. From the way she was looking at me, I could tell that I'd missed a sentence or two, staring at the house.

"Present," I said.

"I hope this wasn't a mistake. Coming here."

"No!" I said.

Yes! my body added, turning up the choke hold a notch.

I pressed on, explaining to Lily, "It's been the most soul-crushing, sleep-deprived week of my life, so if I seem out of it, that's why. It's like I have a hangover, in the sense that I'm hanging over a cliff and not sure I have the strength to pull myself back up."

I should have left it there. But then I added:

"Plus, I had no idea you sold raincoats."

Lily's response was quickly lost to history as Mark, our Patron Devil of Perpetual Irritation, interrupted with a blunt "Are you coming in or what?" Behind us, Gem walked over as the taxi drove off.

"That driver asked for my number," she announced. "I told him it was zero."

"You'd better be careful," Lily said. "He'll think you're an operator."

"We're LOSING!" Mark cried.

"I suppose we should go in, then," Gem offered.

I wanted to stay outside in the night air for a moment. But

48

I couldn't find a way to ask for that, not with Gem steaming ahead, Mark just plain steaming, and Lily looking like she was running out of steam because my mood was sucking it out of her.

"Shall we share some Romanticism?" I mustered, offering Lily my hand.

"I think I like romance more," Lily replied, taking my hand for the short distance to the door. Then we disengaged to go inside.

This house wasn't where Keats had died—that was a room in Italy. But it might as well have been here, because his death at age twenty-five was in the air, on the walls, and in most every word to be read.

My heart started to pound again.

In the lobby there was a life mask of Keats's face that visitors were encouraged to touch. Such a visage freaked me out. I didn't want to touch it, or to have him staring at me. I turned away, only to come face to face with a life-size bust of the poet.

"We're looking for the next clue, correct?" Gem asked Mark. He nodded.

The other team had already gone deeper into the house.

"Let's divide and conquer," Gem said. This time Lily nodded. Gem headed to the room to our left, Lily to the one on the right. Mark disappeared upstairs.

I walked deeper into the house. I knew I wasn't here as a tourist—I was supposed to be on a quest—but the more I read about Keats, the more the clouds gathered around me.

He watched his mother and his brother die of consumption. Then he himself died of it. Only six years older than me.

I looked at his handwritten poems and felt the words like a barrage.

Youth grows pale, and spectre-thin, and dies.

And

When I have fears that I may cease to be
Before my pen has gleaned my teeming brain . . .

And, in a letter he wrote to the woman he loved,

I have left no immortal work behind me—nothing to make my friends proud of my memory—but I have lov'd the principle of beauty in all things, and if I had had time I would have made myself remember'd.

And, of course, his epitaph:

Here lies One Whose Name was writ in Water.

I could feel my body asking

What are you doing?

And it meant: *What are you doing, going to Oxford?*

And it meant: *What are you doing, pretending you're okay?*

And it meant: *What are you doing in this room as the walls close in?*

The walls weren't closing in. But it felt like they were, and that was enough. I went to loosen my collar again and found it already open. The sweat was legion now.

You have to get out.

I pictured my father. The righteous nod he'd give me when I came back with my tail between my legs, like he'd known all along that Oxford was a mistake, that believing in books was a mistake, that going my own way was a mistake. I was never going to be a Future Leader. I couldn't even master Despondent Poet. I was a Once and Future Loser.

You can't do this.

On the first day of our literature class, the professor had asked us to name our favorite author, and when I'd said Salinger, he'd laughed. "American boys who worship Salinger are as predictable as London rain," he'd said.

You can't do any of it.

I thought about Lily, how she'd flown all this way. How I'd basically put our whole relationship in a state of suspended animation so I could follow my foolhardy dream. I heard footsteps on the floorboards above me—probably the other team, but maybe my team was up there, too. I was losing track of how much time had passed. I told myself I'd only step outside for a second.

The problem was: My failure followed me. My failure to play along. My failure to be here now for the people who wanted me to be here.

It was as if Keats was taunting me:

You're alive, and this is what you're doing with it?

Your youth grows pale, Dash. What do you have left?

I was outside the house. I tried to fill my lungs with the night air. I tried to banish the thoughts from my head. But they were stubborn, and instead of leaving, they jumped on the floorboards inside my head. It was cold, and I kept sweating and sweating. I worried they'd see me out here, out front, so I decided to walk a little farther. Hampstead Heath was right here. I'd only be gone for a few minutes. Gem and Lily wouldn't even realize.

What am I doing?

I remembered a question my friend Boomer had once asked me: "My throat is sore . . . do you think I have a sore throat?" In this case, I thought, *I am feeling very panicked. And somewhat attacked. Does that mean . . .*

I took out my phone and, as I walked into the Heath, I googled *Am I having a panic attack?*

The web doctors listed some symptoms for me, and I had plenty of them. Which only made me panic more. I checked link after link. For second opinions. Third opinions. Ninth opinions.

"This is not good," I told the trees.

I considered some of the remedies the Internet provided for a panic attack.

Don't fight it. Acknowledge it.

"But isn't acknowledging it a way of fighting it?" I asked.

I looked at the next suggestion.

Talk to yourself.

"Already covered," I said. "Unless you have something to add?"

"No," I replied. "Do go on."

Next suggestion: *Close your eyes.*

I wasn't sure this suggestion was intended for people

hanging out solo in a park that looked like the perfect night-time strolling ground for Jack the Ripper's minions. But I did it anyway, making the darkness more personal. This lasted exactly ten seconds, until something stirred in a nearby bush and I opened my eyes so I could at least see the fox before it attacked me.

Breathe through it.

There wasn't a fox. Or maybe it was still in the bush. But I took the fact that I was thinking of foxes and not myself as a good sign. Only then I realized that I'd started to think again about myself and my dire situation. I breathed in deeply, then sighed it out. Breathed in deeply, then sighed it out.

Ask yourself: Am I hungry? Angry? Lonely? Tired?

Maybe I should have eaten. Maybe I should have steered clear of Mark. Maybe I should have stayed in New York. Maybe I should have truly napped until the new year.

Picture your happy place.

I was trying to picture the Strand without Mark. I wished he hadn't brought it up tonight, forcing me to get through him in order to truly make it my happy place. But it didn't take me long to get there: Lily and I are in the Rare Book Room, looking at the covers of old pulp paperbacks, reading each other the innuendo-laden cover copy in our most dramatic gumshoe-and-dame voices. It's just an ordinary hour after school, but it's everything I love, right there.

Focus on an object and keep your attention there.

In order to find this suggestion, I had to focus on my phone. I doubted that counted. My phone responded by telling me I only had 10% of my battery left.

Quickly, I turned off the screen. Then I turned it back on so I could text Lily and Gem:

I've gone for a walk. Need some air. Don't worry about me.

My phone must have been as exhausted as I was, because as soon as the message sent, the screen went black.

I cursed for a moment, then looked up and realized I'd managed to get pretty deep into the park without having any sense of where I was.

I cursed some more.

It wasn't that late, but the park was dark and there wasn't anyone else on the paths. The city provided a borealis to outline the uppermost trees with a hint of life outside the tree-shrouds but nothing I could use as a compass point. Instinctively, I took out my phone to check the map—then remembered, put it back in my pocket, and cursed at a near-epic level.

You're lost, my body told me.

And it meant: *You have no idea what you're doing with your life.*

There—there it was. The sentence that had been taunting me the whole semester. The sentence that hummed in the background every time I spoke to Lily back in New York. The sentence that had made me blink and blink and blink when the future tried to look me in the eye.

"I have no idea what I'm doing with my life," I murmured.

Yes, that was it.

It wasn't a relief to say it. It was scary as hell.

I said it again. Then I screamed it out into the foliated darkness.

"I have no idea what I'm doing with my life!"

To which a voice I'd never heard before replied:

"Join the club."

five

LiLY

December 21st

Dear Father Christmas . . .

I didn't know what to say to British Santa. Would he expect proper English grammar, which I'm terrible at? Should I use Ss instead of Zs, like *cosy* instead of *cozy*? Should I end sentences with *innit*?

I hadn't written a letter to Santa since I was a kid. My mother said that last letter I'd written was more of a manifesto, good enough to retire my Santa letter campaigns thereafter. I'd criticized—sorry, criticised—him strongly then, so perhaps he wasn't eager to hear from old Lily again after all these years.

Dear Santa,
    My name is Lily and I'm nine years old. I think

it's wrong that you use reindeer to make your sleigh go. Have you ever seen the horse-drawn carriages that give rides to tourists around Central Park? They make me so mad. The horses are forced to wait outside no matter how bad the weather is. They get rained on, and snowed on, and cars and buses cough fumes on them. They get a lot of rude customers who don't know anything about how to treat horses. Also, the horses don't get paid. Feeding them carrot treats is not compensation and I know this for a fact because I asked my great-aunt's lawyer who represents the NYC Taxi & Limousine Commission. Neigh, the horses do not get anything!

So, I gathered 28 signatures in Tompkins Square Park for my petition to ban horse carriage riding in Central Park. I'll let you know if I'm successful. I am considering creating another petition to ban your sleigh rides. I'm already unpopular at school so don't worry that this new petition will cause me to lose friends.

I'm sure you're nice to the reindeer who work for you, but I'm also sure that if the reindeer were free to make their own choices, they'd choose to run around the North Pole having fun instead of transporting a fat man around the world.

If you want to know what I want for Christmas, it's for you to treat animals the same way you'd want *them to treat you, whether you've been naughty or nice.*

> *Yours sincerely,*
> *Lily*

PS—I would also like a unicorn magic glow lamp.

PPS—What kind of cookies do you like?

"I don't feel like writing a letter to Father Christmas," I told Mark. He'd said we should compose our letters while we waited for Dash to return to Keats House, since Dash had made it clear that he really, really did not want to participate in the letter-writing part of the game.

"Me neither," said Gem. "I'm rather concerned about Dash. He left so suddenly. You know him best, Lily. Should I be worried?"

"I'm sure he's fine," I told her.

I wasn't so sure.

Dash gets weird when he's anxious. Had me showing up here unannounced spurred his very rude behavior, or was it also about his state of Oxford unease? I didn't know whether to be furious or concerned. Mostly, I felt stupid. What I thought had been a romantic gesture in that day's Advent calendar gift to him had been a complete waste—and apparently me showing up in London was not Dash's favorite romantic surprise, either, based on him abandoning me almost as soon as he'd found me.

Mark said, "Clearly Oxford didn't improve Dash's manners. Pretty rude to just walk out with no warning and no explanation."

Gem said, "He's not rude. He's quirky."

I wanted to know if Gem had noticed quirky-rude Dash having anxiety issues when he visited her in London. I asked her, "What do you guys usually do when he visits you in London? Or is he usually too busy studying when he's at your house?"

"We have the most marvelous time!" Gem enthused. "We go to museums, bookstores, concerts. He's a delight. As you know." Mark scoffed. "Although it was a challenge to get him to leave the house for this adventure, I admit. He seemed so *tired*. Probably just exhaustion from the end of term."

"Probably," I said, starting to feel less furious and more concerned. I wished Dash would share with me whatever he was going through rather than just run away from it. *Tired* sounded to me like another word for *depressed*.

My phone rang with a FaceTime call, and while it wasn't the person I most wanted reassurance from—Dash—it was that other person I wanted reassurance from—my brother, Langston. I stepped outside the museum to take the call on the street.

"How's my dog?" I asked Langston as his face appeared on my phone, in the living room at our parents' apartment. Langston lived in Hoboken with his boyfriend, but he was staying at our parents' while I was away to cover my job.

Boris must have heard my voice, because all of a sudden he bounded into the room and then the picture went insane, as Boris charged my brother, and Langston's phone went flying. Boris in New York barked so loudly that the passersby on the street in Hampstead, London, looked at me with concern, as if wondering where this invisible monster was coming from.

Langston finally grabbed hold of the phone, and he put the picture onto Boris. "Down, Boris. DOWN!" Boris kept barking, looking as if he was about to charge my brother again.

I chimed in. "Down, Boris." Boris sat down, but his tail wagged furiously.

"He's going to pummel me again," said Langston. My brother weighs about 130 pounds, and so does Boris.

"No, he's not," I said. "Boris, settle down."

Boris stood up, and the camera followed him walking to his blanket, where he lay down and whimpered. Langston turned the camera back onto himself.

"I think the brute misses you," Langston said.

"How are my other dogs?"

"They're fine." He paused. "I forgot to give Sadie her medication today. I wanted you to hear it from me. In case the doorman reports back to you. But—"

"Sadie the Pomeranian or Sadie the Chow Chow?"

"Sadie the Pomeranian. But—"

"Her medication is homeopathic and it's really just for her owner's anxiety about being away. It's fine." I was annoyed. I'd left such specific instructions. If it had been the other Sadie, it would have been a huge problem. "But Sadie the Chow Chow—"

"—is diabetic, I know. I didn't forget her medication. And what I was trying to say was I remembered about Sadie the Pomeranian before I returned home, so I went back and made sure she got her CBD."

He waited for me to respond but I didn't say anything. "You're welcome," Langston finally said.

I was supposed to thank him? Langston was making more money covering for me for one week than he made in a month working part-time at Trader Joe's. He should be thanking *me*. This windfall would allow him to take off in January to focus on studying for his master's degree comp exams.

"Where's Mom and Dad?" I asked him.

"They're uptown visiting Grandpa. Then having dinner with Professor Garvey while they're in Morningside Heights."

I sighed. Professor Garvey taught in the English department at Barnard. She was an acquaintance of my mother's, who couldn't wait for me to be Professor Garvey's student next year.

"Don't look so panicked, Lily. I'm pretty sure Mom and Dad haven't chosen all your freshman courses. Yet. How's London? How's Dash? Was he surprised?"

"I guess?" I said. I'd put too much anticipation into the big surprise. The actual moment had been a big nothing. I was an idiot for having invested so much emotional energy in it. "He seems off. Stressed."

"I worried it was a bad idea to surprise him. Freshman year is hard enough, and Dash had to adjust to a whole new country, too. Now you're there and he probably feels pressure to entertain you when maybe he just needed to decompress during the holiday."

"He's glad I'm here," I assured Langston, as much as I tried to reassure myself. We just had to realign to these new versions of ourselves, Dash as the going-to-school-abroad, Oxford version of himself, and me as the gap-year, entrepreneur version of myself.

But our coupled version of ourselves was still solid. I didn't doubt that, and I doubted so much. Whether I was meant to go to college as my parents wanted. Whether Dash really belonged at Oxford. Whether the island of Manhattan could survive the rising sea level caused by climate change. Whether good pizza could be found in London, as Dash insisted. But I never, ever doubted Dash & Lily. And not because I was young and naïve, as my parents sometimes said when I expressed confidence in my relationship with my boyfriend.

What can I say? My heart only wanted Dash. It was that simple.

Mark and Gem emerged from the museum, looking for me. I told my brother to hold on.

"We're hungry," Mark said.

"How about that Indian place around the corner," said Gem. "Join us after your call?"

I said, "Do you mind if I don't? I'd love to wander around

London a little. I'll meet you back at your flat later, okay, Mark?" If Dash could just sprint off into nowhere, why shouldn't I? The thought of exploring the city alone at night was intimidating—but so was the thought of hanging out with Dash's grandmother without him there, and pretending to like whatever undoubtedly terrible restaurant she'd chosen.

Gem asked, "Is this a generational thing? Abandoning your elders on a literary treasure hunt?" She laughed at her own joke. I didn't.

Mark grimaced at me. "I don't like leaving you on your own in the dark, in a strange city."

"That's when the fun starts," Gem said.

"Lily will be fine," Langston called out from my phone. "She'll probably have a pack of dogs following her and protecting her within minutes."

"That's true," said Mark. He looked at me like he thought he was my dad or Grandpa. "You'll be okay on your own?"

"Yes," I sighed.

Mark said, "If you're not back at the flat by midnight, I'll be calling Interpol to look for you."

Gem said, "I spent a marvelous weekend in Mallorca with them a few years ago. They so needed a break from Morrissey by that point in their tour."

If I'd learned anything from Dash, it was that Interpol was an international police organization as well as the name of a band, and that while Morrissey was a gifted singer and delightfully macabre songwriter, he'd also become an unfortunate right-wing nutter in his later years. No wonder Interpol needed a break from him. As Dash put it about Morrissey, "There's a light. It went out."

"Bye, guys," I said to Gem and Mark. I returned to my call with Langston. "Where should I go?"

"Where are you now?"

"Hampstead Heath."

"Benny and I went to a great pub in Hampstead last summer. I'll send you a link. Enjoy a pint for me!"

A pub in a strange country was about the last place I wanted to go. I felt anxious and unsettled. However, a pub might be just the place where everyone else felt the same, only happier, because of the beer. I'd pass on the beer but eagerly seek the jolly.

The pub Langston suggested, the Holly Bush, was about a fifteen-minute walk from Keats House, through the center of Hampstead, then up a steep side street. The pub was a series of oaken rooms with stained-glass windows, colorfully wallpapered walls hung with gold-framed artwork, and dark wood furnishings that looked lifted directly out of a Dickens novel. I immediately loved the place, but it was crowded, and I indeed felt intimidated. Then I heard a voice call to me from a cozy—sorry, cosy—corner with a fireplace. "Lily!"

I walked over. It was Azra Khatun, sitting by the hearth, drinking a hot chocolate and reading a book. She said, "Now you've found me in two of my favorite London places—

Daunt Books and the Holly Bush. We must be fated to be friends."

"How can you read here?" I almost shouted. "It's so noisy!"

"I love the noise. I find it relaxing. So much jolly! Olivier hates it. Please, sit down and join me." I sat down next to her by the fire. "Olivier left not long ago, but I wanted a hot chocolate, so I stayed."

"I'm hungry. Is the food here good? Everything here looks so meaty." Everyone I'd passed in the pub seemed to be eating some sort of game. "I'm vegetarian."

"I eat only halal foods so I haven't had most of the things on the dinner menu. But for dessert, I can recommend the sticky toffee pudding."

I approve of people who skip dinner to go directly to dessert. "I've never had that. It sounds both disgusting and amazing. My favorite kind of dessert."

"You'll love it. I'll get us one." She stepped away to the bar to place our order. When she returned, she settled comfortably into her chair, like she was ready for a long fireside chat. "So how long have you and Dash been together?"

"Two years."

"Same with me and Olivier. We met at college."

I was confused. "How could you have met him two years ago at college if you just started at Oxford this year?"

She looked confused for a moment, too. Then she said, "I forgot, I had to explain this to my cousin in America, too. In England, college is where you go after GCSE exams, which are like the end of our version of high school. After GCSEs, if you want to continue on to university, you go to college for two years to prepare. It's like Year Eleven and Year Twelve for Americans."

That made more sense. "Did you and Olivier always plan to go to Oxford together, or did it just work out that way?"

Dash and I hadn't really made a plan our senior year, other than that we'd both apply to schools in the NYC area. And now neither of us went to school in NYC. Maybe we should have made a better plan.

"It just worked out that way. To be honest . . ." Her voice trailed off.

I tried to help her out. "Maybe going to university together is a bit much?"

Azra laughed. Because her emerald-green head scarf covered her hair and neck, her pretty face appeared even more vibrant, uninterrupted. "Maybe," she admitted. "I don't know. . . . My parents say—"

"You're too young to be in a committed relationship?"

"Yes!"

"I call it the whisper campaign," I said. "To my boyfriend's face, my parents are warm and welcoming. Behind his back, they're whispering to me that—"

"You need to see other people?"

"That's the exact whisper campaign slogan!"

Azra said, "Of course, in my parents' case, they mean they'd prefer me to date someone Muslim."

"But they're okay with Olivier?"

"They don't love me dating someone Anglican. But I

think that's more because they don't really like Olivier than because he's not Muslim. What about your Dash? How has it been, living so far apart?"

"Not my favorite," I admitted. "But I've been so busy that in some ways, it's nice not having the distraction of him around. I don't think I ever would have gotten my dog crafts site going if he was around." Then I remembered something Olivier had said at the bookstore. "Did you really not believe Dash had a girlfriend back in New York?"

"I mean . . ." She paused, like she was trying to think of a nice way to say what she was going to say. "He seems like a loner. Kind of morose? Not that he's unattractive, of course. He's quite handsome, actually." I nodded, like, *I know.* "I guess we didn't think of him as someone who wanted a relationship, except with books."

I didn't think she meant the observation as an insult and I didn't take it as one. I couldn't be sour, anyway, not when the sticky toffee pudding concoction arrived at the table between our fireside chairs. It was a sponge cake moistened with warm toffee sauce, with a heap of vanilla ice cream melting off its side. It was so good I was ready to move to England immediately.

"I want to marry this cake," I said. "Sorry, Dash."

"Me too. Sorry, Olivier." I took out my phone to see if there was a message from Dash. There wasn't. Azra must have thought I'd reached for my phone to take a photo. She asked, "Are you one of those people who posts everything they eat?"

"No. I only post dogs or dog-related items. And I'm taking a social media break while I'm here." I felt a little drunk off the smell of everyone else's beers and cheers and the sweetness of the pudding and the warmth of the fire and of Azra. As if I were revealing a big secret, I leaned in and said, "But I'm not going to be one of those people who announces they're taking a social media break. I'm just doing it."

"Going rogue," said Azra.

"Yes!" I hoped Dash didn't drop out of Oxford. If I visited him there, I could hang out with Azra, too. Dash could learn to like her and her boyfriend. He didn't even like Christmas when he met me. Now he's practically obsessed with it.

Her phone buzzed with a text message. "It's getting late and my parents want me to come home. Maybe I'll see you at the next Daunt event?"

"For sure!" I said. "What's your number?" She typed her phone number into my phone and called it, so we'd each have the other's number on our phones.

"Do you think our boyfriends will like us being friends?" I asked her.

She laughed. "Probably not! They're so competitive."

"Should we, like, girl-power fist-bump or something now?"

"Absolutely not. See you again soon, I hope."

Azra left. I sat alone in my pub chair by the fire, completely content. It wasn't just that I'd made a new friend. It was that I'd had an adventure, in a foreign country, on my own, with none of my family present. If sometimes I worried that Dash was suffering from depression, I realized that what I was suffering from was suffocation. From my family. I thought I came to England to be with Dash, but maybe why I really came here was to be away from them. To find my own way.

I knew I'd better get home to Mark and Julia's before he called Interpol to look for me, or to see how they were holding up with Morrissey. But I had one more Daunt task to complete.

I took out the Daunt notebook from my bag and wrote.

Dear Father Christmas,
    Please let Dash be okay, wherever he is. Please let him know how much I love him.
                 Love and sticky toffee pudding,
                 Lily

PS—I'd also love a BritRail pass, and more time to explore England.

PPS—You seem slimmer and less jolly than American Santa. Perhaps you're not getting enough cookies from the Eurokids?

I finished writing and then tossed the letter into the fire.

six

DASH

December 21st

Even if the voice was unfamiliar, when the figure emerged from the darkness, his face was at least semi-familiar. His hair was messy, his nose ring the kind that bulls in cartoons wore, creating a perverse gold smile beneath his nostrils.

When he saw me, he laughed. Then he exclaimed, "As I live and breathe, it's Salinger! I've found Salinger!"

Now I knew why he looked at least semi-familiar: He was in my literature seminar. But I couldn't remember him having ever said a word. Including his name.

He took my inability to respond in stride.

"Oi," he said. "What a right idiot I am. Name's Robbie. But since I acquired that name for all the wrong reasons, you can call me Sir Ian instead."

It was already enough to have my solitary moment of extreme self-doubt paraded into. If he was only going to

70

tease me, I would find another park within which to break down.

"Sir Ian? Seriously?" I spat out.

Sir Ian was unflapped. "Hardly. You should call me Sir Ian, but not out of *seriousness*. You're the one dressed like a toff, so I feel I should at least have the benefit of a knight-hood if we're going to rail against life's meaninglessness."

I felt the need to clarify. "I wasn't railing against life's meaninglessness just now. I was railing against *my own* mean-inglessness."

"Noted. And if you note it as well, it will be duly noted."

Again, I couldn't tell whether he was making fun of me or showing me he was on my side.

"What are you doing here?" I asked.

"I'm out for a walk, trying to reacquaint myself with un-bastardized trees. Which you might have figured from the fact that I'm wearing the clothes that people of our genera-tion usually wear when they go to take a walk. Yourself, how-ever . . . ?"

I had to grant him the fact that my ensemble required some explanation. "I was at a literary scavenger hunt that started at Daunt. Our first stop was the Keats House. It ended up being my last stop as well."

This got an approving look from Sir Ian. "Took your eyes off the prize, did you? Keep up that behavior and you'll never be an Oxford don."

"I think at this point Keats has a better chance of becom-ing a don. I didn't just take my eyes off the prize—I jettisoned my team as well, which contained two people I love and one I would gladly leave to the hounds, had I the chance."

Of course, the moment I invoked Mark, I imagined him smirking at my abrupt departure, telling Lily I was no match for a literary escapade and therefore had won her heart under the falsest of pretenses.

I have left no immortal work behind me—nothing to make my friends proud of my memory—

"Let's continue to walk." Without waiting for a reply, Sir Ian plunged farther into the haphazard copses. I kept step, and he continued to ramble as we rambled. "Historically, when two men, at least one of them avowedly homosexual, meet in the moonlight within Hampstead Heath, it is not for a reasoned discussion of their failures. But I sense if anything's going to speak its name between us, it's precisely that. Am I mistaken?"

This was not the first time that my amiability to same-sex congress had been thus polled. Which was, at least, what I assumed was happening. To make sure, I said, "Translation— you're gay, you thought this might turn into a hookup, but you're realizing we're instead going to dive together into the pit of existential despair?"

Sir Ian nodded. "Something along those lines. Although once I realized it was you, I sensed that carnal assemblage was not an endeavor we were going to pursue. Word of your girl-friend's Advent calendar spread among the classes; mostly it was spoken of disparagingly, but I defended the act as sweet. Granted, this was largely because it reminded me of what my grandmother used to do for me and my sister when we were little, not something I'd want from a lover. But still, sweet."

"She *is* sweet," I said. "I fear I'm bringing the sour."

Sir Ian patted me on the shoulder, as if he'd been around the block a few times whereas I had merely taken a few steps down my front staircase. "Sweet and sour are not antithetical," he assured me. "I happen to think they complement each other nicely."

"I get that," I assured him back. "But I'm also no fun when I'm despairing."

"I think that's healthy."

"You do?"

"Well, it's far better than thinking you *are* fun when you're despairing. Those are the people to watch out for. You can revel against despair, but you should try not to revel within it."

"True," I said.

We came to a bend in the path and veered leftward. Sir Ian seemed to know where he was going. After a minute or so of nighttime silence, he said, "May I ask how you're feeling now?"

The walking was helping. I didn't feel as closed in. And maybe talking to someone other than myself or the trees was helping as well.

"I'm more than marginally calmer," I reported.

"Excellent."

"And how are *you* feeling?"

Sir Ian shook his head. "Like shite, truth be told. I feel

73

I'm supposed to be doing something other than what I'm doing. Which is, I must say, a horrible way to feel."

"It's that bad?"

"Bottom of the barrel, my friend. Choking on the dregs."

I knew I wasn't one to speak; still, I found the sentence coming out of my mouth: "But you're going to *Oxford!*"

Sir Ian let out a mockery of a Waugh-is-me laugh. "Ah, yes. Therein lies the irony. Or maybe therein lies the joke. You see, I fought my way into Oxford with the sole intention of burning it to the ground. Not literally. But I thought I and I alone would be the one to expose the hypocrisies, start the rebellion, throw enough dirt at the pristine walls that at least some of it would stick. I was going to disrupt all the stuck-up, unfair traditions . . . without having any idea that there's already a long line of disruptors who've tried, and are still trying. You know why I didn't talk in class? It was my way of *not being part of the system.* Yes, you heard that right, my newfound chum—I thought the best way to rebel was with *silence!* And do you know what happened? *Nobody noticed.* I at least had the wisdom to know that signposting it—*Hey, world, see how silent I'm being!*—was even more grossly stupid than my original strategy. So I left. I bet you didn't even realize I was gone from class, did you?"

I had to admit I hadn't.

Sir Ian nodded; it was exactly as he'd expected. "I haven't been to school in a month, Salinger. The mental health professionals have been very kind in granting me a 'leave of absence'—as opposed to a 'leave of presence,' I suppose, which was exactly what my first few months at university were. Ladbrokes would not put the odds as favorable toward my return. But that only leaves me with the question of what next. Let me tell you, it's very hard to pick up the pieces when you have no effing idea where they landed."

"Under the couch, in that corner you can't reach," I offered.

"Or out the window, buried by the dog."

While my tone had been joking, his was forlorn. His pieces truly had fallen into unreachable places. Which made me think of my own disrepair.

"I thought I was smart," I said all of a sudden. "I really thought I was smart. But after the last couple of months, I'm not sure. And that's paralyzing, isn't it? To discover you're bad at the one thing you thought you had going for you?"

Sir Ian studied me now—studied me to a degree that nobody I'd met at Oxford had cared to try. "Salinger, you are not striking me as un-smart. If anything, I would rank you among the articulate. And I do not bestow that designation lightly."

"So why are we messing it up? Why aren't we the shining stars of Oxford?"

"I fear we are a hairsbreadth away from bona fide whinge-ing, but I'm going to indulge your question by diving underneath it. Because that question isn't *really* the question you want to ask. You don't really want to be a shining star, do you? You've gotten close enough to those stars to see they shine like gold, not light—light being the thing that stars should rightfully be made of. You're disenchanted with all that, aren't you?"

"Yes," I admitted. I didn't want to be gold. I wanted to be light.

"Scream it."

"Excuse me?"

"Oh, come on. You were perfectly happy screaming before. So scream it now: *I am disenchanted.*"

I hedged among the hedgerows. "It's stranger, knowing that you're hearing it."

"Indulge me."

"I AM DISENCHANTED!" I belted out. Unseen birds flew away in response.

Sir Ian appeared satisfied. "Now: *I am disappointed.*"

"I AM DISAPPOINTED!"

"Good. Now, side question: Have you worked hard?"

So much reading. So much studying. So much worrying.

"I've worked my ass off," I said.

"I suspected so. And because of that, I can point out that your disappointment is directly tied to your disenchantment. It's not that you've disappointed Oxford, Salinger; Oxford's disappointed you. And because you are of a certain nature—a nature I happen to share—you'll be prone to turn that against yourself. Don't."

He made it sound like a simple equation. As if my body wasn't my mind's accomplice in the backlash, infusing me with a panic that broke through the dams of my rationalizations. As if there was a definitive way to protect myself from

76

myself, an armor I could put on without the mind also knowing how to take it back off.

"How have you managed?" I asked. "How do you avoid turning against yourself?"

Sir Ian sighed. "I haven't. I turn against myself all the time. But my advice is still sound. It's easier for a surgeon to treat a patient than to operate on himself."

I decided to share with him something I'd been thinking about a lot lately. It hadn't felt right to talk about it with Lily or Gem—they weren't in the same place I was in, which was another way of saying their minds weren't working in the same way mine was. And the people at Oxford hadn't been that welcoming to my thought patterns, either.

Now I put it all out there, hoping Sir Ian would understand.

I told him, "The one positive thing my father said about me going to Oxford was that it would 'build character.' I imagine that's a phrase that's been used for centuries there. And I believed it. I wanted my character to build. But it's like the message got garbled, and instead of building character, we're all dead set on building *a* character. Like, we have this idea of who we're supposed to be, and *that's* what we're building—no matter whether or not it corresponds to the person underneath. And social media's only made it worse. There, the character building is out of control. You can split yourself off into multiple characters if you want, some of them lovable, some of them attack dogs. I liked to think that I was better than that. That I knew better. But now I wonder if I fell for it just like everyone else, only I happen to be really bad at it. I am a bad actor when it comes to playing myself. What do you do when you discover that?"

"I think maybe . . . oh, I don't know." Sir Ian shook his head, stopping himself.

"No," I insisted. "Tell me."

"It's just so sappy."

"Let the sap run," I said, even though I was mostly allergic to sap, unless Lily was the one tapping it.

"Fine," Sir Ian said. "If I were going to give you more advice that I myself can't seem to take, I would tell you that in order to build character, you don't invent a new self, you instead build on what's already there. The good parts. The things you love. As horrid as it sounds, at a certain point— i.e., the point we're at now—you build your character on the foundation of all the things you love."

The things I love.

I thought:

I love Lily.

I love books.

I love words.

I love my family when it recognizes me.

I love the fact that I am trying hard to learn as much as I can.

I love Holden Caulfield, not because he's a rebel but because he's in so much pain.

I love Seymour Glass even more, mostly because I'm not entirely sure why.

I love the song "Bloodbuzz Ohio," mostly because I don't know what the lyrics mean but when I'm listening to the song, I feel like they fit into my soul in exactly the right way.

I love poetry even if it scares and confounds me a little bit. Okay, a lot.

I love New York so much, especially when I'm away from it and don't have to deal with things like tourists, garbage pickup, and the price of a grilled cheese sandwich.

I love Cate Blanchett even if she scares me a little. Okay, a lot.

I love Carly Rae Jepsen because she doesn't scare me at all, and instead makes me want to dance and feel at the same time.

Those are things I love. Not entirely in that order. But #1 and #2 definitely at the top, in that order.

And then I thought:

So?

I'd kept walking, and when I looked to Sir Ian, he wasn't next to me. I stopped and looked around, but it was all just darkness and leaves.

"Sir Ian?" I called out.

"Don't worry, I'm near." His voice came out of the darkness. "You were thinking about the things you love, weren't you?"

"Yes."

"Good. The fact that it took so long for you to realize I was gone means you have a pretty solid foundation on which to build character."

"But I also have stress and doubt and fear."

"Most human beings do."

"But it overwhelms me at times."

"Just as it overwhelms most human beings. Life, dear Salinger, isn't in the vanquishing, it's in the navigation."

We were far from any lamps, far from any signs of the city. I could hear it in the distance, but so faintly it could have been my mind playing tricks.

"Can you come back out now?" I asked. "It's seriously spooky in here."

In response, he said, "Have you ever been to a Christmas tree farm?"

"Excuse me?"

"Indulge me, Salinger. Have you ever been to a Christmas tree farm?"

In New York City, the closest thing we had to Christmas tree farms were parking lots full of kidnapped pines.

"No," I said. "Why?"

"Do you know what the trouble with a Christmas tree farm is?"

"No. What?"

"It should be a forest. Any assemblage of trees should be a forest. In the same way that trees should not be shoved into the center of your parlor and asked to stand alone. No tree ever grows up wanting to be a Christmas tree. I can almost live with a big tree in a town square; at least there it has its outdoor dignity intact. But to tame a tree and keep it indoors? That's not the spirit of any season I want to be a part of."

"I'm not disagreeing with you . . . but I don't see how this explains why you're hiding in the dark."

"It's the reason I come here, Salinger. Especially this time of year. For a moment, take yourself away from all the Christmas trees and put yourself in the forest. Oxford is a Christmas tree farm, and your time is better spent in the uncultivated wild, making your own stance. You might not get as much attention. You may never shine like gold. But you will grow to be yourself. Be okay with being alone, Salinger. Make sense of it. Figure out what your heart wants . . . then go to it. It's not the gilded prize or the biggest present that we seek, my new friend—it's the forest."

I couldn't say I fully understood this, but there was definitely a door within me that was opening to the understanding, a heart waiting to usher it in.

In the meantime, I had smaller goals.

"Can you at least tell me how to get out of here, Sir Ian?" I asked.

"I'm going to leave you now, but I'm sure I'll see you later," Sir Ian responded. "You're on your own . . . until you're not."

I heard the sound of his departure then—not footsteps, really, but the sound of branches being pushed aside, then falling back into place.

I was alone in a foreign place, in a foreign city. The wind picked up and I pulled my collar closer, tried to stay warm. For a minute, maybe three, I stood there in the center of it all, and as I did, a small piece of understanding came through the door.

Dear Father Christmas,

    I am lost, for sure.

    But there is value in being lost.

    And one of the values is the way being lost can lead you to see what you want to find. It helps you sense where you want to be found. Or who you want to be found by.

"Lily," I said out loud, even though I knew she couldn't hear me.

"Lily," I said again, safe in the knowledge that soon she would.

seven

LiLY

December 22nd

I'll be home for Christmas, if only in my dreams.

My ringtone sang these words as my phone alarm went off at 6:30 a.m. It was a dreamy way to wake up, before my eyes opened, the song conjuring my happiest of holiday visions: Christmas in New York, its bright, twinkling lights under dark winter skies, that first smattering of snow, walking hand in hand across Washington Square Park with Dash, taking in his warmth.

Dash wasn't just a dream. He was real. How lucky was I?

He'd texted me the night before that he was fine after ditching the Daunt event, and he was excited to see me, just the two of us, alone finally, today. My waking heart swelled in satisfaction, but then my body rebelled. *Ouch!* cried out my back. *Motherfrocker!* said my right shoulder. *I hate you!*

announced both my knees. My eyes burst open, and I remembered why my bones were not agreeing with my heart's content. I'd spent the night on possibly the world's most uncomfortable sofa, lumpy and too short for me to sleep with my legs fully extended. Now I was sore and wondering why I hadn't used my dog job earnings to spring for a hotel. I'd considered that prospect, of course, but the prices in London were ridiculous. Plus, staying in a hotel *and* paying for it seemed like something Actual Adults did, not an eighteen-year-old on a gap year who still lived at home. Sleeping on the floor would probably be more comfortable than my cousin's sofa.

I sat up, trying to stretch and twist my body back into place. I had an exciting solo adventure ahead that morning—the real reason for coming to England, besides seeing Dash—and I wasn't going to let a creaky body get in the way. I should have known better than to look at my email on my phone before digging through my purse for some ibuprofen. I saw a message from my mother with the subject line "College Plans," and now I could add headache to my body's aches.

Dear Lily:

Dad and I met with Professor Garvey at Barnard today, and we were very disappointed, to say the least, to learn that you have not responded to any of her invitations to sit in on one of her classes and talk about your freshman curriculum with her. As we've told you many times, most incoming students don't have the opportunity to meet with and talk about their studies with one of the school's most esteemed faculty members. This is not an offer to be taken for granted, and in continuing not to take it, you are giving Professor Garvey the impression you are not interested in her guidance.

I'm also disappointed that you didn't clear out your cookie-baking materials from the kitchen and store them in Langston's old room, as I requested. I spent an hour yesterday boxing all your kitchen items (who needs that many cookie cutters?!) to make room for me to start preparing for our Christmas festivities. I must have asked you dozens of times to take care of clearing out the space before you left for London, but, I know . . . drumroll, please . . . you were too busy walking dogs or designing crafts for and about dogs to take care of this one task I asked you to handle. I really could have used your help getting ready for Christmas this week, too. But, I know, I know, seeing your boyfriend in London was more important.

I do hope you're having a lovely time with Dashiell and I will probably not be so grumpy by the time you return home, but I'm not making any promises. If you want to give me anything for Christmas, please answer Professor Garvey's invitation to you already, and please consider getting rid of all the kitchen equipment you don't need. We just don't have the space.

Love,
Mom

So, two major things happened to my formerly mellow mother in the past year.

Number One is she decided not to move to Connecticut to be with Dad, who got a job at a rural boarding school and lives out there during the week. My parents have a weekend marriage now, which leaves my mother way too much alone time during the week. She uses this time to obsessively peruse the Barnard website to plan my future four years there. I should join the Bacchantae—the same a cappella troupe she belonged to when she went to Barnard! I'll make more friends if I join the Skip Stop Commuter Organization, the organization for student commuters! Mom doesn't want me to live on campus because it's too expensive, she says—but what she really means is she doesn't want to be the primary caretaker for Boris if I live at Barnard. She's so rude to my dog; I would never leave him to live alone with her. When she's not overdosing on planning my future college life, Mom likes to rent a car to go out to the wilds of New Jersey, where she wanders Ikea or Target aimlessly for hours and returns home with more kitchen gadgets, candles, and throw pillows than anyone could possibly want or need. Her other major time suck is she joined a feminist book club led by this Professor Garvey. It's a monthly gathering of students, academics, and randos, where the participants leave the meetings even angrier than they arrived, fired up about economic inequality, patriarchy, and who makes the best chocolate chip cookie on the Upper West Side: Levain Bakery or Jacques Torres. (Only this Professor Garvey is not a Levain supporter, which makes me very, very suspicious of her.)

Number Two is Mom started having major middle-aged lady hormonal changes. And she is moody as frock. See Number One.

We never used to fight, not even when I had my major adolescent girl hormonal changes, but now we fight all the time, although we are not the type of family for loud shouting matches. Instead, Mom delivers a torrent of not-passive-aggressive-enough digs, which I return with silence, rolled eyes, and the occasional slammed door.

God forbid you take your education as seriously as dog-walking, Lily.

I seem to remember having taught you to clean all your dishes and put them away every night so the kitchen is clear for the morning. Did you just forget that habit I worked so hard to cultivate in you?

Our dinner reservation was for six, not six-thirty! It sure would be nice if you prioritized actual time with your parents as much as you prioritize FaceTime with your boyfriend.

After reading my mother's email, I was about to throw my phone onto the floor in irritation when a text arrived from Dash. *You up yet? Want to meet me and Gem for breakfast? She's just discovered avocado toast. She says it's more delicious than David Bowie circa 1975.*

I let out a giggle that felt good to my achy body. I typed back: *I'm free after lunchtime. Meet you then?* Dash texted the thumbs-up emoji back. I added, *Do you want to continue* with the next *Daunt Literary Challenge* clue? Thumbs-down response. Dash added: *I'm a Foyles bookstore man, to be honest.* Before I could be disappointed that Dash wanted to opt out of the game, he sent me a photo of that day's Advent calendar gift to him, along with heart emojis. *Thinking hard on this one,* he wrote.

I looked at the photo he'd sent, of a piece of paper torn from a Moleskine notebook, on which I'd written the following quote from poet Mary Oliver:

Tell me, what is it you plan to do
with your one wild and precious life?

Dear God/Allah/Buddha/Oprah—how I love Dash.

Mark stepped into the living room from his and Julia's bedroom. "Good morning!" I said.

"Coffee," he muttered.

I joined him in their tiny kitchen as he brewed. Mark said, "I bring Julia her coffee in bed. We read our books or the news, when we can stomach it, for about an hour. It's our morning ritual."

"That's—"

"—don't say 'so cute.'"

I mimicked the flat, nasal accent of so many California reality-TV stars. "So cyoot."

Mark gave me the same face of disdain I give to my mother lately. He said, "I have our next Daunt Literary clue. See if your rude boyfriend can be ready to meet us around noon."

"He doesn't want to play anymore."

"I hate dropouts."

"You dropped out of Williams College!"

"To follow Phish for a semester! And then I transferred to Boston University, which was a much better fit for me."

"So maybe that's what Dash needs, too. Just a change in direction. Not dropping out."

"Are we still talking about the Daunt Books Bibliophile Cup Challenge?"

I had no idea. I said, "Dash says he prefers Foyles, anyway."

Mark gasped, as if I had just suggested to a Yankees fan that they could also support the Mets. He looked at me seriously. "Are you Team Dash, or are you Team Strand?"

"I'm Team Lily," I said. "I play to be my best version of myself, so I can be the best girlfriend, the best dog-walker, the best family member—"

Mark put up his hand. "I don't need any more wisdom you probably acquired from a meme."

Since he was already annoyed with me, I ventured, "I'm thinking I might stay at a hotel for the rest of my visit. I don't want to be in your and Julia's way." I'd also woken up to a surprising bank notification that I'd gotten a very generous Christmas tip from one of my favorite dog-walking clients. Suddenly a hotel seemed much more within my financial reach.

Mark sneered. "Yeah. I'm sure that's the reason. Look, I can understand if you want to be alone with your boyfriend. But I have to report back to Grandpa, and if he finds out you weren't staying with me—"

"That's not why," I said. Although it was a very good reason why.

"Don't be ridiculous." He poured two coffees and headed back toward his bedroom. "Family stays with family." He closed the door behind him with his foot.

Family stays with family. It was the reason during my childhood that my parents, Langston, and I crammed into the den every summer at my great-uncle's summer house on the Jersey Shore because the bedrooms were already taken. It was the reason I stayed at the hoarder house of second cousin once removed Louise during my college visit weekend to the University of Pennsylvania—and then my parents wondered why I didn't like Philly! It was why my parents insisted I live at home at Barnard next year—a convenient excuse for not acknowledging the on-campus housing costs were more than they could afford, on top of tuition, or that my mother didn't want her only roommate at our East Village homestead to be a giant bullmastiff.

Family stays with family wasn't the best of our family values—and I was sick of it.

I scribbled a note to Mark and Julia letting them know I was out sightseeing for the day and left their apartment.

After a half hour's train ride from Waterloo Station, I arrived in Twickenham, about eleven miles southwest of London. The town name itself appealed to me. *Twickenham.* It sounded so British, but in this vague way, like it could be either a very posh town or a stereotypical working-class one where people actually said, "Pip pip, guvnah." Once I disembarked and started walking, Twickenham appeared to me to be an affluent town that, despite the so-cyoot houses and buildings I passed on my walk from the train station, was also dreary under the gray skies.

I followed the directions I was given, walking to the end of a long street off the main road, then finding the tall tree with a sign posted on it that said DOGS WELCOME. PEOPLE TOLERATED. Next to the tree was a high wooden gate. I unlatched it and, as instructed, made sure to close it all the way once I was on the other side of it. Behind the gate was a modest two-story thatched house, to my disappointment. I'd hoped Narnia would be on the other side of the gate, not an ordinary English house that looked like so many of the others I'd passed on my walk. I went to the door and rang the bell, which spurred my favorite of all noises—a very loud and excited dog's bark. From a partially open window near the front door I heard a lady's voice call out, "We have company, Innis!"

It was a chirpy voice talking to the dog, so I was surprised when a dour-faced lady, probably in her sixties, with ginger hair streaked with gray, answered the door and said, very brusquely, "I'm Jane Douglas, Head of School. You must be Lily?"

"I'm Lily!"

Her face burrowed more deeply into disapproval. "You Americans always sound so cheerful. It's so unnecessary." She had what I thought was a Scottish accent, based on my many viewings of *Outlander*, and a stern demeanor that suggested treachery, an assumption also based on my many viewings of *Outlander*.

But her dog! A short-haired terrier, a gorgeous brindle of tan and white, about thirty pounds, with a sweet face rather like a pit bull's, greeted me with licks of love. "This is Innis," the lady said.

"What breed is she?" I bent down to greet the mush more properly.

"Staffordshire bull terrier."

"I think she likes me." I certainly liked Innis. Her human? Not so sure.

"Don't take her affection personally. She's like that with everybody. Her breed is exceptionally patient. Their tolerance with people and children has earned them the nick-name—"

"—nanny dog!" I proclaimed, remembering what I'd read about the breed in a book about British dogs.

"I don't care to be interrupted," said Jane Douglas. "But correct. Very good. Come in."

I followed her through the foyer into a living room with glass walls at the back of it, facing a huge yard with a garden and ample frolic space for a pup. The living room had a fire-place, several chairs strewn about, and two sofas that faced each other. "This is where I conduct most of the classes," she said, gesturing for me to sit down.

"Here?" I didn't want to offend her, but this living room was the famous Pembroke Canine Facilitator Institute?

She sat down opposite me, and Innis sat by her side on the floor. "People are always surprised by that. I don't understand why. I only take twenty students per year, and it's much more comfortable to lecture in my own home than at an administrative building."

"But . . . isn't there a facility where students actually get to work with dogs?"

"Of course there is. We partner with a local rescue facility a bit further out of town. They're busy preparing to host the Canine Supporters World Education Conference after Christmas, so I'm not able to give you a tour there today. But as you can see, we have everything we need for learning right here."

"We do?"

"We have a dog right here. We have a yard outside. And we have a rigorous curriculum I've designed myself. Dog behavior—body language and vocalizations. How dogs think and learn. Therapy dog training. Anatomy and first aid."

Again, I said, "Here?" Did Jane Douglas realize we were in a living room?

She said, "The book-learning part of the program we do here. The hands-on dog part we do at the shelter."

I hesitated. I didn't know what to say. This setup was so

not what I expected from the "Harvard of dog schools." I guess that's what happens when you apply to a school you learned about from Reddit comments, one without a website or Instagram page, but with great reviews from British dog-walking enthusiasts. (A subject I became very interested in when Dash decided to go to Oxford.)

My parents would never agree to this over Barnard College of Columbia University in the City of New York. PCFI was only a one-year program, so I could try to sell them on the idea that I'd go to college afterward, but it was going to be a very tough sell.

"What about housing?" I asked meekly.

"You're on your own for that. Several of my students have found housing together, and they often pass down their rooms to the new students when they graduate. Or you may apply for the Pet Store Residency."

"The what?"

"Let's go for a walk and I'll show you. It's an apartment over a pet store in the town center. The shopkeeper offers free rent to one of my lucky students each term, in exchange for tending to the store pets when the store is closed. Let's go, Innis."

I didn't know which option appealed less: going to Barnard but still living at home with my moody mother, or going to PCFI and being "in residence" over a pet store.

The light drizzle had turned to a steadier rain when we went outside, making Jane Douglas's front yard appear even more lushly green, but also dreary. I don't know why, but I loved that. I had this weird feeling like I might actually love a school in a living room—especially if Dash was a train ride away. As we walked back toward town, Jane Douglas handed me Innis's lead.

"Let's see your technique," she said. I took the leash in my right hand so that Innis would walk on my left, with my arm at an angle and my leash hand close to my body with enough slack for Innis to move freely but not so much that she could get tangled. "Nicely done," Jane Douglas acknowledged.

"I'm a professional dog-walker," I told her.

"I know that. I read your application."

"Are there other dogfluencers in the program?" I asked hopefully.

"What are dogfluencers?"

"Dog people with social media followings."

"I certainly hope not. I want students who are here to service the animals. Not who are looking for the animals to service them."

I didn't know what to think. Was this the worst program ever, or possibly a genius learning institute in disguise? "What's it like living in Twickenham?" I asked as we came closer to the main road.

"Some students enjoy the proximity to London. For others, it's not close enough. Twickenham Stadium is the home of England Rugby, so on game days, expect eighty thousand drunk fans descending on the town. We're directly underneath the Heathrow flight path, so also expect jet noise and transportation pollution."

"So far it sounds amazing," I said.

"I like your sense of humor, Lily. And your way with a dog." We crossed the busy road to a path along a park that ran beside a river. "I've told you the not-lovely parts about Twickenham. Here are the wonderful ones. Parks. The Thames. It's not the quaint version of England you might have imagined. But Twickenham has its quirks."

One of those quirks was sitting on a park bench. "Who's that?" I asked.

It was a disarmingly lifelike statue of a lady, seated with a book on her lap and a hat by her side. "Poor dear Virginia Woolf," said Jane Douglas. "She was hospitalized at a nursing home for women with mental disorders here in Twickenham. There's a proposal for a permanent statue of her to be erected, but the funds haven't been approved. A local artist made this mock statue from Styrofoam, to show what the statue could look like." Quotes from Virginia Woolf were painted on large rocks situated on the pavement below her feet.

Lock up your libraries if you like; but there is no gate, no lock, no bolt that you can set upon the freedom of my mind.

Books are the mirrors of the soul.

I thought, of course, of Dash. I thought of how lost he seems to have felt lately.

And I thought, *I know* exactly *what I'm doing with my life. I don't know how I'm going to do it—or if Pembroke will be the place—but I know with certainty: I want a career working with dogs.* I didn't want to go to Barnard.

Tell me, what is it you plan to do
with your one wild and precious life?

What could be a more wild and precious life than one working with dogs and living near Dash? Why should I wait on that until I finished college? That was the life I wanted *now*. So what if the school was in someone's living room? I didn't need to be rich or famous or fabulous and I didn't need a prestigious education to please my parents. I needed to please myself.

Life is so hard. I see it everywhere. I see the homeless people on the street. I see how tragically humans have hurt the earth. How terribly they hurt each other. I also knew how lucky I was. I wouldn't take my privilege for granted.

Truth be told, my parents would prefer me to break up with Dash, even though they like him well enough. *You're too young to know what you want*, they're always saying. To which I say . . . *Really?* Over his parents' objections, my great-uncle Sal married his high school sweetheart when they were just eighteen, and they've been together for over fifty years now, and they have four children, nine grandchildren, great-grand-twins on the way, and a house on the Jersey Shore that's always too crowded but also always brimming with love and laughter. I think they knew *exactly* what they were doing when they were eighteen.

And suddenly, as I looked at Styrofoam Virginia Woolf, I had a vision of what my future could be. It was just a flash, but it was a certainty. My future, at least right now, was here in England. Dreary, odd, wonderful Britain. With my dreary, odd, wonderful Dash.

And the Pembroke Canine Facilitator Institute was quite possibly where I'd forge that future.

On the train back to London, I composed that Christmas present Mom requested, and cc'd her on the email.

> *Dear Professor Garvey:*
>
> *Thank you for your kind invitation to meet me and talk about my courses at Barnard. I'm sure you have amazing insights and I'm truly grateful for your offer. However, I have decided not to go to Barnard after all. I hope someone who really wants to go there will get my place instead. That's who should have it: someone who actually wants it. Turns out, what I want right now is not in New York at all.*
>
>

Yours sincerely,

Lily
>

After I hit Send, I made a hotel reservation for the rest of my stay in London. Like an Actual Adult.

I couldn't wait to return to the city and see Dash and tell him the news. Him! Me! Together in England! But just as I was about to text him, he texted me a photo of a Christmas tree standing in snow-covered Central Park and this message: *I can't wait to go home to New York.*

eight

DASH

December 21st and December 22nd

I wandered for hours until I found my way home.

I plunged headlong into the streets without a phone to guide me. I was no longer in the forest, but I was in a different kind of forest, weaving through the canopy of concrete and glass, largely silent as the night narrowed into sleeping hours.

This was something I loved to do in New York; I'd much rather walk fifty blocks home than entrap myself in the sweaty subway. But in Manhattan I had mastery of the grid, whereas in London I was confounded. I knew the sensation of wandering in the city but not the city itself; I was in a different version of the familiar world, geography in an idiosyncratic translation. Instead of going into a pub and asking for a bit of charge, I decided to feel my way, consulting the rare map that appeared along the side of the road, more for daytime tourists than nighttime wanderers. I knew I had to make it to the river, and eventually I did. Then all I needed to do was make my way to the other side.

By the time I got to the Millennium Bridge, there were still a few late-night carousers around—drunkards wobbling from their ale-ments, couples huddling close to keep their relationships warm, every now and then a fellow fellow dressed to the nines well after twelve. I let them all drift past me like ghosts while I focused on my own materiality, on feeling that I could anchor myself amidst the wideness of this world. On the larger scale, I had no idea where I was going. So best to focus smaller-scale, to know that Gem's town house was my next and best destination.

Still, I didn't go there directly. Even as I made it to the southern side of the Thames, I let my path diverge so I could stay solitary for a little bit longer. What better way is there to clear your head than to stroll in a normally crowded space that's now empty of all people?

I needed that aloneness . . . and then I needed to return from it.

I texted Lily as soon as my phone's charge had returned, and I left a note of apology for Gem on the kitchen table before crashing to a largely dreamless slumber. I awoke the next morning to Gem in my doorway, saying, "Dash, I think we need to have a conversation about manners."

"I'm sorry," I said before opening my eyes. "My spirits died, and my phone followed suit. So I went for a wander."

"I certainly admire the impulse, but I have some quibbles with the methodology." I opened my eyes and saw her looking around my room. "But at least you hung up your suit rather than sleep in it. This speaks to a certain sobriety."

"The only elixir to pass my lips was solitude," I assured her.

"Be careful you don't drink too much of that," Gem warned. "It needs to be balanced by a rich diet of fine company. Otherwise, the benders can be cruel."

"Today shall be dedicated to fine company," I promised. "Starting, ending, and in-betweening with Lily."

"Is she up?"

"I haven't sent my owl over to check." In truth, I didn't even know where she was staying, although I assumed it was with despicable Mark.

"Well, if she is, invite her over for breakfast. The British have done this wonderful thing where they've taken guacamole out of the realm of corn chips and put it on *toast*."

"It's also beloved by young Americans, I'm told."

"How appropriate. Every time I take a bite, I recall Bowie, circa *Young Americans*. And I think, *Somebody up there likes me*."

Before I texted Lily again, I opened her Advent calendar and found an exhortation from Mary Oliver:

Tell me, what is it you plan to do
with your one wild and precious life?

It was a very good question, and rather than try to answer it alone, I wanted Lily's help.

Shuffling into the kitchen, I sent my message and discovered she wasn't free until after lunch. Mercifully, she was willing to break from Mark's feat of literary control-freakery, so we'd be able to wander our own way. (I imagined Sir Ian nodding at this decision.)

Gem seemed disappointed that Lily wasn't able to join us for our morning repast, but she took it in stride and went into the parlor to put *Young Americans* on the turntable. We started to sing along to "Fame" together, me somehow understanding how trapped Bowie felt even though I wasn't remotely famous. Then something tragic occurred—the record gashed itself into a nasty skip, and an already repetitive song got stuck in a rut.

"That's not good," Gem said as Bowie sang *I reject you first* over and over.

Gem pulled the needle from the damage done, and put on Bowie's *Low* as a salve. Returning to the kitchen, she said, "You'll have to run to FOPP to pick up a new copy. I'd do it myself, but I've pledged myself to Liberty for the day. I'm not sure they'd be able to make it through the holiday season without me."

I headed off to the shower (British showers being a somber drip as opposed to a turbo jet), continuing the "Fame" chorus even though the high notes weren't ones I could reach (not even in the shower).

Perhaps it was the thoughts of fame, or maybe it was because my brain had already been wired against my will to pick up my phone the instant I had a free moment. Whatever the case, my mind went back to the notion that Lily had made herself a presence on the Internet—a presence I'd never detected myself. So after clothing myself and seeing Gem off into the day, I went onto Lily's dog-walker Instagram.

I didn't know why I'd never checked it before. I'd been assuming it was utilitarian, the equivalent of a copy-center-multiplied flyer that you'd put up on supermarket bulletin boards. I didn't think there'd be photos—which I immediately conceded was a complete failure of my imagination: I knew this culture, so I should have known that something involving *dogs* would also involve *photos*. Give the people what they like, right? Dogs playing chess. Dogs dressed as hamburgers. Dogs walking into refrigerator doors, then coming back and walking into them all over again.

But that wasn't what her Instagram was like. There were dog photos for sure. But the dogs were never alone. They were always, *always* joined by Lily. Lily beaming as a Jack Russell terrier tries to run up a slide. Lily managing to keep four bulldogs leashed and happy as they pass under the Washington Square Arch. Lily tenderly coaxing a Chihuahua out of a tree. These weren't selfies. And they weren't posed. Lily seemed aware of the camera, but mostly she was aware of the dogs. These photos were posted by other people. Which meant that other people knew who Lily was, and where to tag her.

Which meant that Lily was a celebrity.

Maybe not a major celebrity. But definitely a New York celebrity, which was its own kind of celebrity. The pimple doctor who advertised on the subway. The mayor's third mistress, who seduced the mayor's fourth mistress as an act of revenge. The hairdresser who went a little crazy and shaved his initials into the back of his clients' necks, which was only noticed weeks later. Of course, the initials soon became a status symbol, and rich people paid hundreds of dollars extra to be thus defaced.

And not only was Lily a New York celebrity—she seemed aware of it. Her Instagram led to her dog-walking website. And on her website there was a button marked SHOP. This was where the doggy raincoats could be found. And the doggy sweaters. And the doggy beanies. Not to mention Lily-branded pooper-scoopers.

"This is unreal," I said out loud, because apparently I couldn't keep it inside.

It wasn't like I thought Lily was dig-nostic or e-theist. I knew she was on social media. But I'd kinda thought it was so she could see her friends' cat photos or donate to strangers' kidney drives. In other words, I figured she was on it to see things. Not to be seen.

But that wasn't what this looked like.

I knew I should have been proud of her. I'd known her dog-walking business was a success—but this took it to a whole new level. And even though I fought against it, what I felt when I realized this was . . . loss. I'd thought we were nobodies together. But now I was seeing a somebody. And there was no trace of me anywhere near her.

I scrolled back to the start, but all I found were dogs. Lily, dogs, and New York City. I found myself running to her Face-book profile for consolation, because there we were, right in the profile picture, on a blanket in Bryant Park for a free summer viewing of *Booksmart*. We were both cracking up— instead of asking us to say cheese, our friend Boomer, behind the camera, had yelled out different kinds of cheese himself, taking picture after picture as he cried "Jarlsberg!" and "Pepper Jack!" and "Havarti!" to the heavens until we were having a conniption, mostly at the reaction of the hipster hordes around us, despairing at something so cheesy.

Even as I headed out to wander the streets of London, I kept riding Lily's time machine back to New York. While I walked over the Thames, I thought about the Hudson. While I made my way up the Strand, I thought about navigating the aisles of the Strand. As I stopped by Piccadilly Circus, I was reminded of the circus of Times Square. And while I didn't feel any tenderness toward Times Square itself, I did feel tenderness toward the way its lights would bathe Lily in different colors as she beheld the dazzle of the display. Where I saw crowds, she saw congregations. Where I saw light pollution, she saw light shows. Seeing the place through her eyes didn't bring it to life for me, but it gave it a humanity that I wouldn't normally grant it. And feeling the humanity of the city around you always makes it feel more like home.

I made my way to the Waterstones flagship, knowing that a bookstore in any city could feel like home. Waterstones did not disappoint. But even as I retreated into the comfort of shelf-talkers telling me which titles various booksellers had recommended, I still felt too much of a remove from the city of my heartbeat. In rushing off to Oxford for a more formal education, had I stepped too far from all the things that New York had taught me? I'd been happy enough to move away from my parents, but weren't Lily and Boomer and Dov and Yohnny and Sofia and all my other friends part of my family as well?

I can't wait to go home to New York, I texted Lily. Then I added, *It's been too long.*

When I didn't get an immediate response, I reached out further.

In the meantime, be a Young American with me.

Then I sent her the link to FOPP's closest location.

If our hard drives are ever wiped out by an electrical pulse, a place like FOPP will be indispensable for the restoration of our culture. Records lined the walls and both CDs and DVDs lined the aisles. In other words, it was a haven for those of us who wished we were back in 1994. Beneath people's parkas there were plentiful glimpses of flannel and band T-shirts. All of the staff members looked like they played in bands, or at the very least did light design for bands. Stevie Wonder sang from the rafters, signed, sealed, and delivered straight into our hearts. I couldn't think of any better ode to joy for this holiday season.

From what I could tell, Gem's record collection went no later than the later works of George Michael, so while I waited for Lily, I picked out some Decemberist and National records for her Christmas present. Then I went over to

Bowie and found a pristine remaster of *Young Americans*. As I flipped through all of his albums, his glance traveled around the room—eyes up, eyes down, side glance, straight-on stare. It was as if he never wanted to be photographed the same way twice. Here was a person of his own invention. I had to admire that, and wonder how I could get there myself.

"I once had a babysitter who would show us *Labyrinth* every time she came over," Lily's voice said from somewhere close behind me. "I was never sure whether David Bowie was a Muppet or a god. I didn't know he was a singer until Langston started getting into his music. When I asked him what he was listening to, he showed me the album, and I said, 'Oh! The guy from *Labyrinth*!' He thought that was hysterical."

I turned around and gave her a kiss. Then I said, "Gee, my life's a funny thing."

"Why?" she asked.

"Oh," I said. I held up *Young Americans*. "It's from the title song."

"I guess I have some catching up to do."

She started sifting through the records in the row next to Bowie's. The song overhead shifted to "Wonderwall." Her face lit up. "Oh," she said, "I know this one. And love it. Though I still don't really know what a wonderwall is."

"That's what's so perfect about it," I told her. "He's made up this whole word for how he feels about the person he loves. The line before it, saying maybe you'll be the one to save me, is what defines *wonderwall*."

"Well, in that case, you're my . . . songloop."

"And you, Lily, are my joypill."

We flipped through records some more.

Casually, I said, "I saw your Instagram."

She kept flipping through the Bs and Cs. "I haven't posted anything in days. It's the same as last week."

"Yeah. But that's kinda what I'm trying to say. I've never actually looked at it before."

Lily picked up a Brandi Carlile record, then put it back. She looked Brandi in the eye, not me, when she said, "Okay . . ."

It was starting to feel like a mistake to bring this up. I said, "It's not that I wasn't interested in you. You see that, right? It was *because* I was interested in you."

This got Lily to look at me. "You didn't check my Instagram because you were interested in me?"

"I'm interested in the in-person version of you," I explained. "Not the . . . *creation* that's on there."

This was not the right thing to say.

"How is that *creation* not me?"

"No! It *is* you! I know that. But it's not—" I stopped myself.

"It's not what?"

"It's not the you I love."

Triple-wrong thing to say.

Lily put the Brandi Carlile record back, then faced me fully. "Dash, I know you think you're better than the Internet. There's a part of me that absolutely loves the fact that you want to write letters instead of emailing, and hold off on

108

seeing each other until we can actually see each other face to face. But when this Dash comes out, the one who can only see me if he's looking down his nose at me—well, let me put it this way: That is not the Dash I love."

"Fair," I conceded. "Totally fair."

"You're not the judge! Of anything!"

"Of *anything?*"

"No. Because your opinion matters too much to me!"

When you hit quadruple wrong, you basically have two options: You can dig in until you end up buried . . . or you can put your shoulder to the wrong and try to move it in the other direction.

"I'm sorry," I said. "Nothing is coming out right. I'm trying to confess something to you; it isn't meant to come out as an accusation. What I'm trying to say is that this part of your life that was abstract to me before is now full of specifics. Your life has flashed before my eyes and it's not a view that I'm used to. I am a private person. I have always been a private person. You are the only person I have ever let wholly into my privacy. And I guess my way of seeing that, of getting used to that, was to think that you'd come into the privacy with me. That we were there together. But that required a very selective blindness on my part. Because this whole time, you were building something out in public. I knew it was there. I love talking to you about it. But it hadn't occurred to me that I was able to see it from afar."

"It's just pictures, Dash. Pictures of me and my dogs."

"I know, I know. That's what social media is: the fronts

of the postcards, rarely what's written on the backs. I wanted the full postcard, Lily. But as a result, I missed out on seeing where you were. Because that's what the front of the postcard says, even if it isn't personal."

"I wasn't sending you messages on my Instagram. I know you're not on there. I know that's not how we communicate."

"But it's a part of your life, isn't it? And it would be easier for me to see if I were on there. If I were a good boyfriend who checked his girlfriend's posts."

"Stop. Really. If that was what I wanted, do you think I ever would've started dating you?"

I was about to say *Fair, totally fair,* but I stopped myself.

Lily smiled. "It's okay. You can say it."

"Nope. Not gonna say it."

"Did you follow me?"

"I'd follow you anywhere."

"Not true. And I meant on Instagram."

"I don't have a profile anymore. Thus, cannot follow you. I'm content to be your number one lurker."

"Be sure you sign all your valentines that way."

"Maybe I can buy my valentines on your website. I recall seeing something heart-shaped."

"Those were treats."

"I can get them engraved. *A special treat from your number one lurker.*"

"If you do that, I'm getting you a collar for Christmas."

"Kinky."

"Ew."

"Look, I can buy these another time. Let's venture out. London awaits!"

"I thought you wanted to be back in New York?"

"I want to be with you. And since you're here and I'm here, let's make the most of our temporary city and the wild and precious day."

I knew Lily would love Covent Garden, with its ornament stalls and ever-present carolers. We turned into the area around Seven Dials, stopping for ice cream at a place called Udderlicious. It was only as we were sitting at the table, licking the salted caramel (her) and the black cherry (me), that the sheer ordinariness of what we were doing hit me, as well as how it hadn't been ordinary in what felt like ages.

Lily saw me pause.

"What?" she asked.

"You're here," I said. "You're really here."

"Where else would I be?" she replied.

But I knew she had plenty of other places to be. I knew so well all the things she brought to my life—calm and sweetness, nerve and verve. But what did I bring to her?

I could feel myself start to stress.

No, I counseled myself. *Enjoy it. She's here. This can be the rest of your life.*

"You're quiet," Lily observed.

"Not in my head," I told her. "Never in my head."

"Let me in. I want to hear it."

"That's not the voice I want to be using to talk right now," I said. "Yours is truly the only voice I want to hear. Tell me about your day."

She told me about the dog-handler Harvard she'd visited; I bristled at the sound of the word *Harvard* but could tell the program had made a good impression.

"But it's not like you need to go to dog-walker grad school," I said. "I mean, you're like the Megan Rapinoe of dog-walkers. I've known that about you since the week we met. And it seems like the secret is more than out, if the testimonials in your Instagram comments are to be believed. And since they were all impeccably spelled, I am inclined to believe them."

"There's always something else to learn," Lily said.

"I think you mean there's always too much to learn," I countered. "Or at least that's true for me."

Once our cones were licked and eaten, we decided to take the side alleys rather than the main streets. It was only as we neared Covent Garden that we stopped with some alarm.

From around the corner of our somewhat narrow mew, we heard a terrifying bark. It sounded like a basset hound was auditioning to play all the young girls in *The Crucible* and had just spotted a trio of witches cavorting in a cauldron. It was pain and euphoria in a single howl, mangled with bursts of ferocity and contention.

"Oh, no!" Lily cried. Then she broke into a run.

Most people go running in the other direction when they hear a rabid cry. Not my girlfriend.

I rounded the corner close at her heels. It suddenly felt like all the streetlights had been turned on and aimed into our faces. I moved my arm up to block my eyes, but Lily kept going.

"It's okay," she started saying. "C'mere, it's okay."

"CUT!" a human voice yelled.

I took my arm down from my eyes. I saw Lily in front of me comforting a mega–German shepherd. And behind her there was . . . a camera. And a crew of about a hundred people. And a very irate director.

"WHAT DO YOU THINK YOU'RE DOING?" He didn't need a bullhorn to sound like a bullhorn. "WHO LET YOU—"

Then he stopped. Looked at the mega–German shepherd docile in Lily's arms.

"How did you . . . ?"

A young man with a headset slid next to me. "We've been trying to calm that dog down for days," he confided. "Her trainer is worthless. This is the miracle we've been praying for."

Lily looked a little flustered when she realized what she'd interrupted. But mostly she was concerned about the dog.

"What's her name?" she asked the director.

"Daisy."

The name meant nothing to me. But Lily looked gobsmacked.

"Like . . . the Daisy who starred in the movie version of A Dog's Porpoise?"

"One hundred percent that bitch," the director confirmed.

It was clear that his leading lady had chewed his bones for too long.

Three very glamorous people gathered around.

"This is unreal," one of them said. The other two nodded.

"Co–executive producers," Headset Guy whispered to me.

"What does that mean?" I whispered back.

"I don't know. It's like having silver status on an airline. Gets you a slightly better seat, but it's not, like, a major accomplishment."

"Are you a professional?" one of them asked Lily.

Lily didn't hesitate. "Yes."

"Are you free for the next two hours?"

Lily looked at me and I nodded.

"Yes," she answered.

The movie was called *The Thames of Our Lives* and apparently told five interconnected stories of Londoners falling in various forms of love as New Year's approached. In this particular vignette, Daisy was playing a hapless romantic who'd died in a freak disco ball accident . . . only to be reincarnated as a dog who manages to insinuate herself into the household of the hapless romantic's equally hapless sister. Now the dog was trying to set the sister up with the man she'd loved all along but had never had the courage to ask out. (The sister was being played by Serena Forrest, an American actress with a winsome range and a fulsome accent. The love interest was being played by Rupert Jest, an actor from the Royal Shakespeare Company no doubt looking to subsidize his husband's touring production of *Matilda*.)

The scene they were shooting was not, to my understanding of the plot (such as it was), an important one. The sister and the suitor had just suffered a street-corner spat, and had exited in different directions. Now the dog needed to choose which of them to follow.

This won't take long, I thought. All they had to do was film a dog looking both ways, and then eventually going right. Lily was expert at coaxing such a performance with neither howl nor umbrage. *Twenty minutes tops,* I believed.

But no. The director thought Daisy didn't have enough conviction . . . and then she had "two shades too many." Between each take, the dog's fur had to be recalibrated. When there was finally a take that the director and producers found satisfactory . . . they would try again, just in case they could get it better. And then, after ten or eleven shots like this, they took twenty minutes to set up the cameras to face the dog from a different angle.

I turned to Headset Guy, who'd told me he was a "PA"—I wasn't sure whether this was in some way related to the state of Pennsylvania or an indirect way of saying "pa." I asked him, "Wouldn't it be easier to move the dog?"

"Do you need me to get you some water?" he replied.

Passersby kept craning at the barricades that had been erected, trying to witness some of the action. But the action was minimal, and they soon retreated as boredom pushed them away. I had no such luxury—when Lily stepped out for a second to take some tea, Daisy protested with a snarl that made Big Ben wet his pants a little. Lily hurried back, and the talent licked her joyfully.

I tried to ingratiate myself with the crew. It apparently took two hundred people to film a single dog, so I had many crew members to choose from.

I sidled over to the guy holding the long pole that led to the microphone over Daisy's head. He kept it aloft for a superhuman amount of time, his arms unwavering, with the solemn, determined expression of a Buckingham Palace guard.

"I imagine people must come up and tickle you all the time," I said to make conversation. He somehow managed to shift away from me without moving the microphone an inch. This led me to believe that people did not, in fact, come up to him all the time to do that.

I spotted a woman who was wearing an apron covered with tools and wires.

"Got any Twizzlers in there?" I inquired. Then, realizing my mistake, I added, "Red Vines?"

She, too, shied away.

"Do you have any idea how much longer this will take?" I asked the PA once we crossed the two-hour mark and the director was trying to explain to Daisy her motivation for looking right.

"Are you sure I can't get you some water?" the PA replied, then walked away.

Eventually I wandered far enough to get to the craft services tent. The shoot had clearly run its course, because all I found were a few distaff stumps of celery, a smudge of hummus at the bottom of a bowl, and a dozen servings of chamomile tea.

I wandered back to the set. Lily was having to stay just out of frame . . . but still close enough for Daisy to find her there.

The trio of co–executive producers came over.

"Are you her manager?" one of them asked me.

"I'm her boyfriend," I explained.

The second co–executive producer sighed. "You should never hire your boyfriend to be a manager."

"Better than your mother," the first co–executive producer said.

"Yeah, I guess it's better to hire your boyfriend than your mother."

"Oh, I wasn't using that generically. I meant your mother *specifically*."

"Holy cow!" the third co–executive producer cried, holding out his phone. "Take a look at this!"

It was a picture of Lily and Daisy, looking like lifelong friends.

"Serena tweeted this out—" the third co–executive producer said.

"She knows she's not supposed to post any images!" the first co–executive producer lamented.

"Shush!" the second co–executive producer countered.

"Look at those comments! Apparently, our dog whisperer has quite a following herself. And Daisy's and Serena's respective fans are in love."

The third co–executive producer broke into a wide grin. "Ladies, gentlemen, and those who defy such categories, I'm happy to announce . . . we're *trending*."

He said this like it was a good thing. The best thing.

But I wasn't sure it was a good thing at all.

nine

LiLY

December 22nd

I didn't even know his name and he was propositioning me.

"Do you want to work on *The Thames of Our Lives?*" asked the same fast-talking producer with the American accent who'd just announced that we were trending. But he was also on a phone call. To someone on the other end of the call, he barked, "Have her circle back to me ASAP." He tapped the AirPod in his ear and looked at me, like, *Well?*

I have two second cousins and one third cousin once removed who work as film crew, and two former aunts who are actresses (that uncle who married them has a type), and so I happen to know a person does not get randomly hired on a big movie or TV production without a lot of layers of decision-making, paperwork . . . and a union. I don't belong to a union and I'm not a scab.

I told the producer, "No, I don't want to work on your

movie. I want you to take responsible care of your show animals! Whose dog is this? The trainer's who ran off?"

The producer shrugged. Another producer of unknown rank appeared from nowhere, this one with a British accent. "Daisy's my dog," she said.

I said, "The trainer you hired to work with Daisy was obviously not prepared for the job."

"Ya think?" said the American producer with the AirPod in his ear.

Dash leaned into me and whispered, "Is he talking to you or someone on his phone?"

I had no idea.

Daisy's producer human said, "Job's yours. And we'll throw you on-screen to add social media appeal. We can only offer scale but with bumps based on engagement on your socials."

"No, thank you," I said, before I remembered a better, less polite industry term I could have used: *hard pass*. Then I called out to the dog who would have been my set charge and could have been my scene partner. "Daisy!" Daisy bounded toward me. "Sit," I commanded her. She looked reluctant and confused. Who wouldn't be with dozens of film crew and strobe lights that could power a skyscraper directing all their attention at her? Luckily, I was wearing my Lily Dogcrafts coat with the treat pocket sewn into the inner liner. I pulled out a baggie from the treat pocket. "Sit," I repeated to Daisy.

She sat. I gave her a handful of treats and then I got down

on my knees so that she and I could have a heart-to-heart, head-to-head.

"Is it time for the Vulcan mind meld?" Dash asked me.

I still wasn't sure exactly what the Vulcan mind meld was, but I knew it involved some TV show Dash's mother loved, and that it was what Dash called my solemn talks with dogs whose humans I perceived to be less than responsible owners. "Yes," I said to Dash. Then, to Daisy, I said, "Shake." She held out her paw to me and I shook it with one hand and then, with the other, delivered a few more treats to her. I stroked her sweet head and then gently spoke into her ear. "Daisy, I need you to behave. You're a big girl and a mighty force. I need you to harness that energy for the good. Not for the chaos. I recognize that your human is less than competent in helping you in this area, so I'm going to need you to do the work. Be a responsible citizen, Daisy. Can you do that? Shake if you agree."

Daisy slobbered a kiss onto my cheek and then raised her paw for another shake. I shook her paw again, delivered a final round of treats, and then kissed her wet nose. "Good girl, Daisy." Daisy's producer human was holding an iPad. To her, I said, "I know someone in Twickenham who could probably help you find a good trainer. Would you like me to put her email address into your iPad?" The British producer nodded.

I typed Jane Douglas's contact information into the iPad and returned it to the British producer. "Aren't you a *macher*," said the American producer to me, then walked off as if we'd never met.

I turned to Dash. Sometimes when I look at him, it's like I want to melt. He wears my heart on his face. "Show me London? Finally?"

He grinned and made a pocket of his arm for mine to latch into. "M'lady," he said.

We had started to walk off the set when one of the main actors, Rupert Jest, came rushing toward us. "Lily Dogcrafts, is it?" he asked me. "I've seen your IG. Marvelous!" He had the kind of posh accent like maybe his cousins worked at Buckingham Palace. It wasn't a clipped royal accent from *The Crown*, but like one of those characters on the show who are always coming into the Queen's private quarters to deliver solemn news and address her as Majesty. Dash and I stopped walking and Rupert Jest handed me a large brown envelope. "If you're not too busy tomorrow, I'd be honored if you and any friends you want to invite were my guests at my husband's production of *Happy Chrimbo, Dick Whittington*." To Dash's and my bewildered faces, he explained, "It's a pan-tomime. A theatrical performance that's a British tradition at Christmas, often based on fairy tales or historical figures. Dick Whittington was a legendary London mayor and also a popular subject in British mythology. We've taken some liberties with the story, given it some modern gravitas, but still good fun. Please come."

I took the envelope from him. It was thick with unsold tickets. "Thank you," I said, trying to be polite.

"We'll try," said Dash, in a tone I knew to mean, *I'd sooner play Pictionary all night with Lily's dreadful cousin Mark and his new wife.*

Rupert Jest said, "And please, do feel free to post about it." He murmured, "Serena refused to post in support. She's just awful, to be honest."

No wonder they needed a dog to salvage their screen chemistry. The star-crossed lovers of *The Thames of Our Lives* had none offscreen.

"I wonder what that's like, to not like someone you work with," I said to Dash as we passed by huge billboards for *The Thames of Our Lives* on the Embankment.

I snuggled tightly into Dash. My happy place. We were on a Thames River boat cruise, which Dash had told me was the most efficient, and relaxing, way to see the most tourist destinations in London without actually having to go to any of those destinations. (Therefore, more time for book and record stores, museums and libraries, strolling through parks and shops, and eating ice cream and English chocolates.) Within a matter of minutes on the riverboat, I'd seen the Houses of Parliament, Westminster Abbey, Big Ben, and the London Eye, which Dash mercifully did not take me on for an aboveground view of London because he knows I'm scared of heights and prone to vertigo and nausea. Seagoing, however, was pure joy. I loved the chilly air, the wind, the sights, and especially having Dash all to myself, my head on his shoulder. Then the Tower of London appeared in the distance and I thought of the horrible things involving heads that happened there, and I placed a grateful kiss on Dash's precious neck.

"If it's anything like going to school with people you don't like, probably not so fun," said Dash.

"Do you hate Oxford?"

"Not at all. I'm just not so sure I've found my 'tribe' there."

"Where do you think your tribe is?"

"I wish I knew."

"Who are your tribe? Besides me, of course."

"Thank you for not saying #SquadGoals. In New York, I feel like I knew the answer to that question. Here? Gem, and that's pretty much it. So far."

I love my family, but I'd probably be bummed, too, if my one human connection in the place I'd most longed to live turned out to be my grandmother. If only Dash liked dogs more, he wouldn't be struggling so hard. I said, "You've only been here a few months. You just need more time to find your people. If I decide to go to Pembroke, I'll be close by. Would that help?"

I wanted him to say, "If you were here, that would make everything right. It would be a dream come true." Instead, Dash said, "Or, you living here would distract me so much that I really never find my way."

In my fantasy of living in England, close to Dash, I hadn't considered that angle. I knew he was right and just being honest, but I also felt slighted that his first instinct wasn't to proclaim extreme enthusiasm for my potential move closer to him.

I asked, "Would it make you happy if I came to school here, too?"

"It wouldn't make me *un*happy."

That was a distressingly dissatisfying answer. "Are you saying you think I wouldn't like it here, or you might not like me being here?"

We untangled and faced each other. He appeared taken aback. "I didn't say either. I'd love it if you were here. I'm just not sure if *I* want to be here. And living in a foreign country is harder than I expected. You're so used to your comfort zone in Manhattan. Your family. Your dogs. I worry you'd have a harder time acclimating here than you think."

"You're saying I couldn't hack it?"

"I didn't say that at all!" He kissed me, mostly to shut me up, I'm pretty sure. But I enjoyed the kiss anyway. Fantastic. When our lips parted, he said, "I wanted so badly to come here, but it's not as great as I thought it would be. I don't want that to happen to you. Just think it through, is all I'm saying." He paused, then added, "Although knowing you, so long as you have dogs near, you'll be fine no matter where you go. I wish I had that ability."

And I loved him even more all over again.

Dash's phone buzzed and he took it from his pocket to look at a text. I had turned my phone off, wanting to savor my time with Dash—and avoid the torrent of angry emails and texts from my parents about my decision not to go to

Barnard. I'd deal with that when I got home for Christmas. For now . . . no. Happy bubble.

And so quickly it burst. Dash said, "Boomer and Sofia are in London! On a layover before catching their next flight, to Barcelona. They want to know if we want to meet up. They didn't know you were in London until they saw you were trending!"

"Oh," I said. Deflated. I adore excitable Boomer, but he sucks up all the energy when he's around. I mostly like Dash's ex, Sofia, but sometimes her impossible beauty and effortless cool are insufferable. (Yes, I am that petty.) I had so little time with Dash before I had to return home for Christmas. It was hard enough to share him with Gem.

"They asked if we want to meet them at the Barbican."

"What's that?"

"It's an arts place, like Lincoln Center. They have music, theater, and film shows. Cafés. An amazing library. Brutalist architecture."

"Brutalist architecture? I didn't even know that was a thing. What is it?"

"Exactly what it sounds like."

"Is it okay if I don't want to go?" I wanted a date night with Dash. Not a double-date night with his ex at a brutal-sounding place called Barbican.

Dash's face fell. "Yeah. Of course." But he was clearly disappointed.

"Guess what?" I hoped my alternative plan would excite him even more.

"What?"

"I reserved a hotel room for the rest of my stay. I can't take another night on Mark and Julia's couch."

"Really? Where?"

"Claridge's." I'd been hearing about the hotel since I was little from my great-aunt Ida, whom my brother and I always called Mrs. Basil E., after our favorite childhood book. It was our aunt's favorite hotel not just in London but in the world, and she'd regaled me with so many stories of its Christmas splendor that I basically had no choice but to book it. I am usually so frugal, and when I got home to New York, it was going to be an epic fight with my parents, so why not enjoy a Christmas splurge while I could with my unexpected client Christmas bonus?

Dash laughed. "No, really. Where?"

"Claridge's!"

"*You* paid for it? Or was this Mrs. Basil E.'s idea . . . and credit card?"

I was offended. "I used my Christmas tips from dog-walking clients!"

"That's one of the most expensive hotels in London! How much money in tips did you get, exactly?" He didn't look as impressed as I thought he would. He looked horrified.

"About as much as three nights in the cheapest room I could get at Claridge's."

Once again, Dash did not take the opportunity I'd practically thrown into his face to proclaim his enthusiasm for my being in London. He said, "That's such a waste of money. You worked so hard for those tips and just blew it on a hotel?"

I spoke before I thought. "Well, it's not like you saw me at Daunt Books and said, 'Gem insists you stay with us!'"

"What are you saying? That I wasn't happy to see you? Gem's house is small. I don't even know her that well yet. It'd be weird to ask her to invite you to stay. I didn't know you were coming!"

It was a good thing I didn't stop to think, because rational thought had no connection to the irrational feelings bubbling up from my burst bubble. "You wish I hadn't come! Everyone in my family said I shouldn't surprise you, and they were right! You'd rather spend Christmas with Gem. And Boomer and Sofia!"

I didn't know how the conversation had gone so downhill so fast.

Dash took a deep breath. Then he said, "Of course your family said their Lily Bear shouldn't come. They'd love for us to remain apart."

And now he was insulting my family? (Even though what he said was true?)

I hadn't noticed the boat had pulled into a pier until a loudspeaker voice announced, "Last call, St. Katharine's Pier, Tower of London."

Dash was right. I had a lot to think about—and clearly I shouldn't be talking because I had turned the loveliest boat ride into a major fight with no provocation. My family would all be furious with me by now. For choosing my boyfriend

over them at Christmas. For choosing the possibility of sharing a life in England with my boyfriend and forsaking their
academic dreams for me to do so. Maybe I wanted to go to
dog school in England and maybe I didn't. It was such a huge
choice. I was overwhelmed and suddenly so, so tired. I really,
really missed Boris.

"I think that's my call," I told Dash. I dashed over the
plank to the pier while Dash remained, mute and shocked,
on the boat. It pulled away.

ten

DASH

December 22nd

I'd been preparing my next sentence carefully while she jumped to shore.

I thought that was what you were supposed to do when you loved someone: If you start to disagree, prepare the sentences more carefully, in the hope that they will take you back to a better place.

You don't cut and run.

So I was pissed. And at the same time, I wasn't at all pissed, because I knew that Lily would never do something so dramatic if she didn't feel she needed to.

I knew I was right about her family. Mark was just an extreme manifestation of how they all felt. They didn't like me. They *tolerated* me. For the most part. I'd won over Mrs. Basil E. as much as she'd allow herself to be won over, and Langston and I had shared enough good times to feel that there'd be more good times ahead . . . but that was two relatives out of a community of at least two hundred. (There honestly wasn't any way to keep count.)

Still, being right and saying it out loud? Two different things.

Same with the hotel. What I meant was: *There is no reason to spend so much money on us being together because I would be just as happy in a roadside Motel 6 with you as in a fancy London hotel. If we start equating the amount of money we spend with the amount of love we feel, we're just as doomed as the rest of the world.* Which was true. But not what she needed to hear at that moment.

I couldn't help but think: *I can't believe she thought that would impress me. Doesn't she know me at all?*

And then I couldn't help but think: *Maybe she really wanted to stay at Claridge's with you, Dash. Maybe that's her fantasy. Don't you know her at all?*

It was all very confusing. Certainly enough confusion to last for the remainder of a tour boat ride.

I texted her repeatedly:

I'm sorry. My point was that we don't need fancy hotels or your family's enthusiasm in order to have the best Christmas ever.

I'm really hoping that if Brexit pirates in Boris Johnson masks hijack this ship and insist on declaring it its own country, you will call in the hounds and save me.

I am taking from your lack of response that I am still causing you distress rather than joy. I'll stop now.

. . . Except to say that I'm going to head to the Barbican to meet Boomer and Sofia and I hope you'll be there too.

I know only the most lovelorn poets quote the Beatles, but I will conclude with this thought: We can work it out.

It was immediately clear upon my arrival at the Barbican that neither Boomer nor Sofia had heard from Lily. I knew this because Boomer's first words to me were "Where's Lily? You can't show up without Lily!"

Sofia, more to the point, asked, "What happened?"

And just like that, I felt like I was back home in New York. Even though we were in front of the Barbican instead of the Whitney or MoMA, we were together, and the city we were in was incidental.

Boomer was the one person I texted semi-regularly from Oxford. I knew that it would be folly to expect him to ex-change letters—I wouldn't have been surprised to learn that he believed that mail magically appeared in one's mailbox and didn't require any effort on the other end. He was now a first-year at the University of Colorado–Boulder, and was enjoying it (after getting over his disappointment that the whole school was not in fact located on a giant boulder).

Sofia and I hadn't been in touch much. We'd developed the kind of friendship where we knew we'd talk when we talked, and if months went by without that happening, we'd be fine. If we needed each other, we could always break the glass and ring the alarm. But it would take a real fire for us to do that.

Now the look in her eyes let me know I should be checking my smoke detectors to make sure they're working.

"She'll show up," I non-explained. "I know she wants to see you both."

"That's why we took this popover!" Boomer said.

"*Layover*," Sofia corrected with a smile. "We have three hours, then we head to Barcelona so Boomer can meet my whole family for the first time."

"But we still have time for the entirety of London's history?" Boomer asked.

"Of course," Sofia said, nodding to a sign that would lead us to the Museum of London.

Boomer was so easy to satisfy. I envied that.

Sofia was much less easy to satisfy, which was one of the many reasons I hadn't believed it when they first got together. But somehow it worked. And now here they were, after a semester of him at Boulder and her at NYU, taking it to the next stage.

I wished I'd had two years to prepare for meeting Lily's whole family. But that hadn't been an option.

"So did you have a fight?" Sofia asked. "Otherwise, it means that Lily doesn't actually want to see me and Boomer."

I felt trapped into answering. "Yes. Although I'm not sure I'd call it a fight. More like a flare-up that ended with Lily running away from me and not answering my texts."

"Well, that's no reason to miss me and Boomer." Sofia took out her phone and presumably shot Lily a text. When the phone was back in her pocket, she said to me, "What was it about?"

"It was about us not reading each other well. The details are almost beside the point."

Sofia nodded, understanding.

"Relationships are measured in dog years," Boomer said.

"Excuse me?" I asked.

"It's a theory I came up with," he continued. "Just take how long you've been together and multiply it by seven, and that's how old your relationship feels. The first year? You're toddlers and then young kids, enjoying things and also slowly figuring them out. Then you get to where we are, around the second year? Adolescence, man. It's awkward, there's rebellion, and most of all you're just trying to figure out the relationship's identity, right? Then around years three and four you get your jobs, you start to really work it. Hit year seven, middle age kicks in. But if you keep going, get to year ten—you've made it to old age. Maturity. And the cool thing is, you don't even die when you get to year fourteen or fifteen—no, when your relationship really works, it can live until you're hundreds of years old. Couples who've been together fifty or sixty years? They're Yoda, Dash. They're totally Yoda."

We entered the Museum of London. Inside, London's history was mapped out for us, and we could begin at whichever spot we wanted. A guard warned us we only had a half hour until the museum closed.

"The fire!" Boomer cried out. "I want to see the Great Fire, and the cow that caused it."

"I think that was the Chicago fire," I told him.

"Maybe they were all caused by cows," Boomer countered. "The Chicago cow was the only one stupid enough to get caught."

"Fair enough," I conceded.

Boomer headed Fire-ward, which gave me and Sofia more of a chance to talk.

"I can't believe the two of you are still together," I said. "It makes no sense."

Sofia laughed. "The same could be said of you and Lily."

"Well, maybe Lily and I aren't going to end up together. Maybe we're mismatched."

"No, no, no," Sofia said. "A mismatch is the only kind of match that's worth making. Surely you know that by now. Are Boomer and I alike? Not at all. Are you and Lily practically the same person? Oh, no. And thank god for that. A match is two separate things coming together. Otherwise you're not a match, you're . . . a *set*. Two identical spoons. Boring."

"Haven't you found it hard, though? Especially being so far away?"

"I miss him a lot. And we text and talk all the time, so he never feels that far. But I'm also happy to have some distance, to feel that I'm becoming myself without having to worry if the relationship is exerting too much influence. It's good to have each other, but you also need to have your own people, your own experiences."

"And you feel you've gotten that?"

"To some degree. I mean, it's always to some degree, isn't it? Hopefully being in love takes you out of the realm of all or nothing. But, yes, to some degree I feel we have our own things. When we first started dating, do you know that Boomer wanted to learn Catalan? So he could be able to talk to my family and my friends from home the same way I did. But I asked him not to. Because I liked having a language that he didn't understand, that I could have to myself and share with people in my own way. It wasn't about excluding him—all of my family and all of my friends speak English, too. It was about making sure that there was something important that remained mine. I figured Oxford was the same for you. But that hasn't worked out, has it?"

I hadn't told Sofia anything about my semester. "How do you know that?" I asked.

"I've been getting reports."

"Not from Boomer. I've been telling Boomer everything's great."

"No. I actually went to boarding school for two years with Azra Khatun. When she first told me how antisocial you were, I wasn't very concerned. *That's my Dash*, I thought. But when she told me you looked miserable, even in your lit classes . . . I knew something was wrong. Which is why I wanted to stop off here to see for myself."

"And how do I look?"

"Not miserable. Just a little lost."

"Did you know that Lily was coming? She surprised me, and I think maybe a little preparation would have helped things go smoother."

Sofia shook her head. "None of us see Lily very much anymore. Partly because we're in school and she isn't. But that's not the only reason. I think she's been keeping her distance, too. She spends much more time with dogs than she does with people, Dash. I'll text her to try to make plans, and I always end up talking to her while she's walking a dog in the NYU area. She looks a little lost, too."

"She's very successful, you know. As a dog-walker."

"I've seen. But I don't think that's the only thing she wants, Dash. It can't be."

We'd now caught up to Boomer in the Great Fire of London room, which featured a model of 1666 London. It all looked normal . . . until the voice-over intoned that the Great Fire started at Thomas Farriner's bakery on (no lie) Pudding Lane. From there, it spread—and so it spread over the model as the walls around us simulated flames and the voice-over provided further facts.

"They should've never let a cow in the bakery," Boomer said, shaking his head as the inferno destroyed the city. "Any word from Lily?"

Sofia and I checked our phones again. No word.

"Their reunion didn't go quite as planned," Sofia explained to Boomer.

"Like ours?" Boomer asked.

"No, not like ours," Sofia said tersely. "That went wrong in a different way."

"What happened with yours?" I asked.

"I told her I was flying into LaGuardia from school, but it was really JFK," Boomer said. "Then I went to LaGuardia to meet her, but she'd already gotten an Uber to JFK. We kept missing each other! I thought it was funny. She didn't think it was as funny."

"I may have been angry when we finally both got to the same place."

"I thought she was going to break up with me!"

"And honestly? I almost did. Because he didn't seem to see what was wrong with what had just happened."

"But I got her to laugh about it."

"Not really. Instead he made me realize I had a choice: spend the rest of the night angry, or put that aside to have a good time."

"I would've probably spent the night angry," I confessed.

"Naw, you wouldn't have," Boomer said. "Not with me all in your face about having a good time."

The simulation ended with all of London in flames. Then the flames retreated, the lights went back to normal, and the whole installation reset.

"We should try to warn them this time," Boomer said.

I shot Sofia a look.

She shot me a look.

Both of the looks meant: *Well, that's silly.*

But then the fire started in Thomas Farriner's bakery, and we were right there beside Boomer, yelling, "Fire! Fire! Get out!" to all the other houses in the model, until a less-than-amused guard chased us away.

The next gallery covered the Expanding City—basically, London rebuilding after the fire and making its way slowly toward the *Downton Abbey* years. Boomer particularly enjoyed the Vauxhall Pleasure Gardens, where various mannequins were dolled up into their most high-society selves.

"Ooh, I like that look," Boomer told one mannequin in a top hat. Overhead, the museum's PA told us politely to exit because the museum was closing.

"I miss hanging out," I told Sofia. "You know, when it's not an effort. When it's just friends. I don't have that at Oxford."

"Azra says you haven't tried very hard."

"Well, Azra probably learned her Oxford hanging-out skills at *boarding school*," I said. "I was thrown into the pool while most of the people there seemed to have been born swimming in it."

"Doesn't matter, as long as you know how to swim," Sofia pointed out. "And you, my friend, know how to swim."

"I swim better in New York," I said. "The water's nicer there."

"A statement that's never been made before, ever. Unless you're talking about what comes out of the tap."

"You get my point, though. I want to go home."

"So go home."

A guard came up and told us the museum was now closed and it was time to egress.

"I guess we'll have to go straight to the present!" Boomer said, heading straight for the door.

Outside, it was complete darkness, December having made away with all the daylight while we were inside. Sofia checked her phone for the time, then typed out a quick text.

"Just because she's mad at you, it doesn't mean she shouldn't respond to me," she grumbled.

"Do we have time for Bad Egg?" Boomer asked.

Sofia checked her phone. "Yes. But we need to be in a cab in an hour if we're going to catch our plane. And since our luggage is going to be on it, we really should catch our plane. It's the last flight of the night."

"Can't let your family think I'm a flight-skipper," Boomer said as Sofia led us on, checking her phone the whole time.

"How are you feeling about meeting her family for the first time?" I asked.

"I'm terrified . . . in a good way." Boomer grinned. "But that's love, isn't it?"

I thought about it for a second before concluding, "Yeah, maybe it is."

Bad Egg was a brunch place that stayed open well into the night. It felt incongruous to order huevos rancheros in the heart of London, but that didn't deter Boomer.

"The stomach wants what it wants," he said. Then, in addition to his huevos, he ordered a Christmas Pudding

Sundae, which involved brandy-soaked fruit and something mysteriously referred to as *Christmas pudding pieces*.

I got a shakshuka and Sofia got a burger, and after our server left, I looked at the two of them sitting across from me, and it just got to me . . . in a good way. This was what I'd stepped away from when I was at Oxford, and what I'd tried to put out of my mind, because it made my loneliness that much more pronounced. I'd thought, for my higher education, that I'd wanted scholarship and erudition. But really, I'd just wanted to have people to sit across from at a diner, to talk about whatever was on our minds, Brontë sisters or Jonas brothers, Carl Van Vechten or Carly Rae Jepsen.

"Are you getting misty?" Boomer asked. Then he put his arm around Sofia. "Look—he's really getting misty."

"I just . . . I've missed you guys," I said, wiping my eyes. Which felt far too mundane an expression of what I was really feeling, which was that I'd jumped too far from the bedrock of my life, and now I was lucky enough that it had come to me rather than waiting for me to return to it.

"We've missed you, too," Boomer said.

"Like the deserts miss the rain," Sofia chimed in.

I couldn't help myself. "Hasn't that line always bothered you?" I had to ask. "Why can't the desert just be a desert?"

Boomer backed me up. "He has a point."

"Fine," Sofia said. "Like the polar ice caps miss the cold?"

"Topical," I said.

"Timely," Boomer agreed. "Or like my stomach misses the sundae that isn't here yet . . ."

Thus began a metaphoricalympics among the three of us, which lasted a few minutes until I sighed.

Reading my mind, or maybe just being of the same mind as me, Boomer said, "She should be here with us."

"Yeah," I said. "She should be here."

"Agreed," Sofia said. "Let's all tell her that at the same time."

We got out our phones and typed out the text: *You should be here*. On the count of three, we hit Send. Then we did it three more times.

No response.

We talked and laughed and bantered over that non-response. Sofia was starting to get nervous about getting to Heathrow, so we got the check and paid it.

It was only as we were getting our coats on that Sofia's phone buzzed.

Sofia had a surprised expression on her face as she read the text that had come in.

"Is it Lily?" Boomer and I asked at the same time.

Sofia shook her head. "No, it's Azra. And you're not going to believe where she and Lily are right now."

eleven

LiLY

December 22nd

You've ruined Christmas, Lily.

When I finally had the courage to look at my phone, this was the first text I saw, from my brother. But it wasn't entirely a disheartening message. Next, he'd written:

Mom is so mad at you that she says she's canceling Christmas this year. No present exchange, no lounging in PJs all day, no Christmas brunch. Hurrah, I say! It's one stupid day of the year! It's ridiculous we spend so much energy and money on it. I've had it with the crass consumerism and awful sweaters. I've been waiting my whole life for Christmas to be canceled, although I certainly never expected our family's #1 Christmas nerd would be the reason why. Now I can spend the day with Benny's family without Mom's guilt trip about me splitting my time between my boyfriend's family and ours. Because Mom's the one who canceled Christmas—her idea! Truly, Lily. You're a genius. And

TBH, the food at Puerto Rican Christmas is better than ours. But your cookies still rule. (I still think you should go to college. Even if it's not Barnard. Let's talk?)

As I walked from the Tube to Mark and Julia's apartment to get my stuff, I ignored the text from Dash—*What just happened?!?!?*—and only glanced at the angry texts from my mother, as if I was taking mental screenshots of only her most vehement points.

If you think you're not going to college you're . . .

Pick up the phone, Lily!

Four generations of women in our family have gone to Barnard. You will not be the first who . . .

But it was the text I'd snuck a peek at half an hour earlier, when I was still on the boat with Dash, that had prompted me to make a run for it. It was from Dad.

You've broken your mother's heart, Lily.

I didn't know what I'd been thinking, jumping off that boat. It was a sudden jerk move, like baiting Dash into a fight had been. I just felt so overwhelmed and lost. How had a day that had started so promisingly, with me taking a step into independence and seriously considering forging that independence in this exotic new place, gone so awry, so quickly?

Because I was a coward, that's how.

I was a coward who knew all along she didn't want to go to Barnard but let her mother think she did. I was a coward who let her mother know via email that she wasn't fulfilling

144

her mother's college dream for her—and with a cc'd email at that. (Coward *and* schmuck.)

I was a coward who surprised her boyfriend at Christmas when she knew he really needed the holiday break for introspection and decompression from Oxford. I was a coward who hadn't considered that she'd be a distraction to her boyfriend establishing his own roots in England if she also moved there, to be closer to him.

I was a coward who flirted with the idea of going to an obscure dog school in Twickenham, England, which would require her to give up the lovely and loyal dog-walking clients who counted on her in Manhattan, and to move away from her own beloved dog, Boris.

Coward coward coward. Jerk jerk jerk.

In the moment, when I sent that email to Professor Garvey, it seemed like a good idea. An act of defiance but also— what's the word everyone uses now?—*agency*. I was owning my power to make my own decisions and choose my own destiny. But in that moment, I didn't think about the consequences. The collateral damage.

I couldn't wait to be in a hotel room alone that night. I needed the introspection and decompression time just as much as Dash. I hoped Mark and Julia wouldn't be home when I returned to their place, so I could get my stuff and make a stealth exit, like the coward I was. But when I went inside Mark and Julia's apartment, I found Mark lying on their dreadful sofa, reading a Martin Amis novel (Mark's love for this author being yet another reason Dash distrusted my cousin). When he saw me, Mark folded the book shut and sat up.

"Now you've done it," he said.

"I know. I got Christmas canceled back home. I'm a monster," I said as I made a mental inventory of my stuff. I'd left my toothbrush and toiletries bag in the bathroom. My clothes were all within an arm's-length radius of my back-pack, shoved behind the sofa to be out of the way of my hosts. At least I'd had the foresight to travel light. I could be packed and gone in five minutes—maybe ten, max, if Mark really gave me a hard time about daring to vacate his crappy apartment for a luxurious hotel because *family stays with family*.

Mark said, "Family crisis back in New York. They're try-ing to blame me for luring you to London. But don't worry. I made sure your parents understood that Dash is to blame, not me."

"*I* am to blame! This is all me. Dash had nothing to do with it."

"Sure," Mark said, disbelieving. "The Daunt Bibliophile Challenge was also canceled. Too many people dropped out. Julia is devastated. I blame Dash for that, too. He started the attrition."

I said, "Blame timing it at Christmas! People are too busy! She should do it in January, when the Christmas lights are gone and people are bummed by winter and really looking for something to do." Like, basic common sense. "And stop blaming Dash for everything."

"You used to be so sweet before you met him. So easy."

"I'm still sweet and perhaps you mistook polite for easy."

Mark stood up from the sofa. "I liked tween Lily better."

How nice of Mark to make such a nice opening for me. I said, "Tween Lily could fit on your sofa for a night's sleep. Adult Lily cannot. I've come to get my stuff and then I'm going to a hotel."

Mark gasped. "Traitor!" Before I could defend myself, Mark's TV rang with a Skype call. The caller ID said GRANDPA.

"Please, Mark," I pleaded. "Wait to answer till after I go."

"Absolutely not, traitor," said Mark. "I texted them when I heard your key in the door. Seems everyone is trying to reach you but you're not answering calls. Not a problem here." He pressed a remote to answer the call. "Hi, Grandpa!" he called to the screen as my grandfather and brother suddenly appeared on it. They were in Grandpa's room at the assisted living facility in Morningside Heights.

The biggest proof of my cowardice?

I had seriously considered leaving my grandpa! My dearest grandpa, who counted on my almost-daily visits to take him for walks around the neighborhood when he was up for it, or to sit by his side and read to him when he wasn't. My grandpa, who loved all his children and grandchildren, but me the most. Then there were his fellow residents, who

147

counted on me to bring Boris around to their rooms for companionship. My fearsome-looking dog had a surprising knack as a therapy animal. He's a simple dude and it turns out the three loves of Boris's life are peanut butter treats, me, and old people.

I started to bolt but Mark muttered, "Sit!" As if I were Boris, I immediately heeded the command and sat. I practically fell into the middle of the lumpy sofa as Grandpa's and Langston's faces looked at me accusingly.

Grandpa said, "So I hear you've gotten Christmas canceled, Lily Bear?" I tried to look away from Grandpa's face, but all I saw were all the family photos surrounding him—at least half of which were photos of me at previous years' Christmases. What a jerk, that cute Lily of Christmases past.

"Where's Mrs. Basil E.?" I asked. It was her day at the home, not Langston's.

Langston said, "She asked me to cover for her today since I'm already in the city. She's also canceling her annual Christmas party this year. Those of us who appreciate her sharing her superior champers collection are hoping for another opportunity on New Year's Eve, or we will be very angry with you indeed."

"Where'd she go?" My heart hurt even more. My great-aunt's Christmas night party was the annual highlight of our family gatherings. Canceling that felt much more dire than canceling presents.

Grandpa said, "Who knows with my sister? She likes to disappear. Now listen, Lily. We can handle your mother canceling Christmas." He stood up from his bed and stepped into his walker, as if to remind me of his fragility. Then he shook his fist at me. "BUT I WILL NOT TOLERATE YOU ABDICATING COLLEGE!"

Langston moved to Grandpa's side. "Seriously, Lily. What are you thinking?"

"I don't want to go to Barnard." Finally, I'd said it aloud, and not just a million times in my own head.

From behind me, Mark said, "God forbid she slum it at that prestigious dump."

It pained me how right Dash was about Mark. My cousin really was awful. He was my family and I loved him no matter what. But he was kind of the worst.

"And what would you presume to do instead?" Grandpa asked.

There was no use being anything other than honest about my intentions. No matter how I answered, they wouldn't like it, so I chose to tell the truth. "There's a dog-training school I got into. Here in England."

Dead silence.

Then Langston said, "What's it called?"

"Pembroke Canine Facilitator Institute," I said.

Mark said, "You've got to be kidding me with that name. Is Barbara Cartland the headmistress?"

"No, Jane Douglas is," I said.

"How'd you find out about it?" Langston asked. "One of your dog-walking clients?"

Quietly, I said, "On Reddit."

Not quietly enough. Langston, who had been sipping water, actually choked on his sip. Then he said, "Lily. Come on. I can understand if Barnard isn't the college for you, despite the convenience of it for everyone else and, um, wait, oh, right—and that it's an amazing school with, like, a seventeen percent admission rate according to Google. That would indicate a lot of outstanding people really want to go there." *Shut up, Google*. I didn't say anything, so Langston added, "But wanting to go deeper on your dog skills is NOT A REASON NOT TO GO TO COLLEGE AT ALL."

Grandpa said, "Agreed. Lily, tell me. What do you think you want to do with your life?"

That was such a big question and there were so many answers. I wanted to be with Dash. I wanted to be in service to others somehow. But above all, I knew: "I want to work with dogs, Grandpa. Maybe become a veterinarian?"

I didn't think I really wanted to be a veterinarian, but it sounded very cool and like something a non-schmuck, totally responsible and mature person would state as a career desire.

Grandpa said, "I believe you'll need an undergraduate degree for that."

"Or a dog entrepreneur," I said. "Dog-walking, dog crafts. That doesn't require a degree."

"But a business education sure would help," said Grandpa.

Langston said, "Do you want to go to dog school in England because of Dash or because it's the right school for you?"

"Maybe both?" I said. Maybe neither, I realized. This

morning, I thought I was so clear on what I wanted. Now this family ambush had me so confused. I had me so confused.

"I've tolerated this Dash long enough. I won't have you moving to England for him," said Grandpa. "I see why your mother is so angry."

"It's not your decision or hers to make," I said. And finally, I said what I should have said to them all a very long time ago. "Dash is not someone who should be *tolerated*. You *tolerate* mediocre pizza or the subway running late, not people who are precious. Dash is here to stay. He's the love of my life. I'm sorry if that makes you uncomfortable because you're not ready for your Lily Bear to fly the coop, but it's a fact. And you should feel lucky I have someone like him for a boyfriend. Because he's good, and kind, and funny, and wonderful. And he loves me for who I am, not for who he wants me to be, like you're doing right now."

There was a long silence.

Then Grandpa said, "How about this, Lily? Don't close the door on college—a *proper* college, not a Reddit whatsit—until you get home and we discuss it as a family. Will you do that for me? And I'll promise not just to tolerate Dash, but accept him. I eventually did it for your father. I guess I can do it for Dash, too."

Grandpa looked so old but not at all frail, and I knew this was a battle I would not win by making a unilateral decision. There was agency—and there was family agency. I cared about both. "I will," I said.

"Thank you, Lily Bear. Merry Christmas," he said, and blew me a kiss from his side of the world.

"Call Mom," Langston said. "Put her out of her misery."

"I will," I promised. I would. Later.

I took the remote from Mark's hand to end the call. Before I could power off, Mark said, "She thinks she's staying at a—" but I pressed the Off button before he could really rat me out. The rat.

I needed to apologize to Dash. Making out with him would be the best way to make up and would make me not sorry at all for what a jerk I'd been.

But my phone would not cooperate with my heart's desire. After I left Mark's, I tried texting Dash. *I'm so sorry. Where are you?* Every text I sent him bounced back as undeliverable. I tried tinkering with my phone settings. Same error messages. Yet I was able to receive texts from Sofia and Boomer.

From Sofia: *I don't know what happened, but I trust that you're right and Dash is wrong. Forgive him and come join us before Boomer and I take off for Barcelona!*

From Boomer: *Where are you, Lily? Did a pack of dogs abduct you? If they did, where did they take you because I definitely want to see the doghouse for abductions?*

Then I got a text from both Sofia and Boomer. *You should be here.*

Where are you? I texted Dash again. Undeliverable again.

I was about to text Sofia and Boomer back since Dash's and my phones were clearly not talking to each other, when I got a text from Azra Khatun. *I have an extra ticket for Hyde Park Winter Wonderland tonight. Want to join me?*

I may have been the reason Christmas got canceled in New York, but in London, I was ready for it. I maybe never needed it more. *Yes!* I answered. I made a quick stop to drop off my backpack at the hotel, then recalibrated my destination to Hyde Park, and promptly forgot to answer Sofia and Boomer.

Finally! FINALLY! CHRISTMAAAAAAAASSSSSS!

"I'm so glad you could come," said Azra as we strolled the most epic winter wonderland ever. In an annual tradition perhaps designed to make me fall in love with London even more, the city's version (to my mind) of New York's Central Park—Hyde Park—was converted into a winter wonderland for the holidays. There were fairground rides lit with twinkling fairy lights, a Santa's grotto where elves and the fake fat man himself held residence, an actual ice slide for the kiddos to freeze themselves silly on, quaint Christmas markets, a circus, a huge outdoor ice rink, and a faux–Bavarian Village with music, food, and merriment. It was like Disneyland for Christmas. I was in heaven. I couldn't decide which attraction I wanted to experience most; I was so content just to walk and experience the spectacle. Cheers to you, London! Azra added, "I'm surprised you weren't with Dash, though?"

"I'm surprised, too," I said. "We had a little fight. My fault. I keep trying to text him, but it keeps bouncing back."

"It's like the universe knows when couples need a break, I guess."

If Dash knew how badly I wanted him to accompany me to the wonderland's screening of *Love Actually*, one of his most hated movies, our relationship could turn rockier. I said, "Hopefully it's just a temporary break. I definitely plan to make up with him. *Hard*." I wanted to buy him a beautiful sweater. He wore them so well, but I enjoyed ripping them off him even more.

Azra laughed. I was in awe of her. She knew about places like Hyde Park Winter Wonderland, and she could stroll that huge park wearing skinny jeans and high-heeled shoes like it was nothing. I wouldn't last one block in shoes that chic and pointy. "I'll miss that," Azra said. "The making up. I broke up with Olivier this morning."

I stopped walking. "Seriously?"

She kept walking like she wasn't perched on five-inch daggers. "Seriously. That's why I had the extra ticket for tonight."

"What happened?"

"I just decided I didn't want to be in a relationship with him anymore. We've been more or less together for nearly two years, but suddenly, this morning, I woke up and thought, *I'm done*."

"Just like that?"

"It had been building for a while. Us going to Oxford together wasn't the best idea. We both could have used more space. What finally did it, though, was we were talking on the phone late last night, as we often do, and he was talking about his aunt who is very proudly antifeminist. He was telling me how this aunt loved me because she said I wasn't one of those young 'woke' feminists. And I said to Olivier, 'But I am a feminist. I don't know if I'd describe myself as "woke," but I try to be aware and respectful of others,' and he cut me off and said, 'You can be empowered and woke, but if you wear a hijab, you're not a feminist.' And I thought, *Does he even know me at all?* I told him, 'Wearing a hijab is *exactly* what makes me a feminist. It's freedom of choice. My choice. It's a modesty that expresses humility and respect. It's a reminder of my community. It's a reminder to believe in myself and what I stand for. What's more feminist than that?'"

"Like self-esteem based on your relationship with God?" I asked her.

Now she stopped walking. "Yes! I let it go when I talked to Olivier last night, but I was bothered. I barely slept. And this morning, after I showered and put on my scarf, I knew. It was over."

"Are you sad?"

"Yes. And relieved. He's a lot of work, that Olivier. He's hypercompetitive, a bit pretentious. We're about to go into a new year and I don't feel like carrying that energy of his into it."

"Are your parents happy?"

"They were surprised and tried very hard to disguise their glee."

I spied the entrance to the Bavarian Village nearby. "I think you need some delicious German treats. How about some lebkuchen cookies, my treat?"

"And a mocktail to go with them, please."

We headed in that direction. I said, "I don't know how you walk in those shoes. Do your feet hurt?"

"No. A girl I went to boarding school with, who did some modeling, taught me how to walk in heels. I've just been texting with her, actually. Your Dash's ex, Sofia—"

"You know Sofia?"

"Yes!"

"You never mentioned you knew her before."

"It never came up before. Does it matter?"

It really didn't matter, and it was silly of me to feel jealous, once again, of perfect Sofia, whose skill set I'd now learned included modeling, and not only wearing high heels but mentoring others in how to do so. "Nah," I said. "Was she perfect back then, too?"

"She was naughty! She had a Swiss boyfriend that she used to sneak out and see after curfew. She wouldn't get back to our dorm until, like, four in the morning. I was such a proper girl and I was so scandalized and impressed. Then her family moved to New York and she dumped him. But the poor fellow. I don't think she told him she was moving, because he would come to the dorms in the middle of the night and stand outside yodeling for her!"

"Yodeling ironically or for real?"

"We honestly never knew."

Somehow this story made me like Sofia. And reminded me I still hadn't answered Sofia's and Boomer's texts. But I was too distracted and delighted to bother with texts now. Azra and I had walked inside the Bavarian Village, which was strung with lights and filled with people laughing, drinking, and eating, and there, before us, was my Holy Grail of Christmas: a carol-oke bar for singing Christmas carols!

A waitress dressed in Bavarian costume approached us holding a tray shaped like a long ski, with container holes that had—"Shotski?" she asked us.

Azra said, "I don't drink. Lily?"

"Sure, why not?" I said. The legal drinking age in England was eighteen. Enjoying this drink now could be like time-traveling to my twenty-first birthday in New York. The party would be legendary and could start now.

"Five quid," the waitress said, and handed me a shot glass filled with a Scotch-colored liquid from the ski tray.

I gave the waitress a £5 note and took the glass. I didn't sip it but drank it just as instructed—as a shot. And it felt like one—a shot directly to my heart, warming my body and reminding me what this Christmas had been missing for me all along. SONGS!

Three, four, five shotskis later—I don't know, I lost

count—I was the star of carol-oke and had a crowd of merry-makers joining me, with Azra laughing on the sidelines. I was perched center stage with a giant screen behind me broadcasting my face to the whole park as a new song came onto the carol-oke monitor. I sang aloud into the microphone.

It's the most wonderful time of the year . . .

Before I could sing the next line, the microphone was grabbed from my hand. By Dash. Looking not happy at all, but scrumptious in his favorite old peacoat.

"Is it?" Dash asked the crowd.

twelve

December 22nd

It was, frankly, time for Hyde Park to go back to being Jekyll. Because the holidays had brought out its most festive beast from within.

At first, the state of Lily's sobriety or lack thereof wasn't entirely clear. Because, truth be told, Lily was a girl who could get completely drunk on caroling, no liquor needed. All it took were a few jingling chords for her Little Drummer Girl to take over the beat, and after that, it was all goodwill hunting. When she got into that zone, all I could do was step aside and give in to the sheer harmonious delight of it. Did I stop to observe the irony of a group of people loudly asking *Do you hear what I hear?* when their voices would clearly drown out any other sound? Sure. Did I think the proper answer to the question *Do they know it's Christmas after all?* was "Don't you think it's problematic that you're rating their problems

159

on a scale of a holiday that many of them don't even celebrate? Don't you think the lyric *And there won't be snow in Africa this Christmastime* is possibly the most ridiculous piece of condescending, colonialist crap that has ever been committed to vinyl?!" It's possible that thought has crossed my mind once or twice. But did I keep those thoughts inside and let the music fill the night without my commentary? Yes. Because I appreciated the spirit in which it was being sung.

So after I saw Boomer and Sofia off . . . after I made my way to Hyde Park amidst people wearing plush antlers without any sense of shame . . . after I found Lily by hearing her voice take a solo on "Santa Baby" . . . at first, I was inclined to hold off on any humbug. I wasn't even peeved that the screen behind her would soon be showing a certain holiday "classic" (its title should really be *Love . . . Actually Not*).

No, what Scrooged me over was the fact that as Lily was out in front, giving a new song her all with a proclamation of the "hap-happiest season," there were three drunk Santas behind her, elbowing the more earnest carolers out of the way and pretending to grab Lily's ass.

Now, I knew there was no way I was going to be able to take on three drunk Santa bros without having to be carried away on a sleigh, so the best I could do was move Lily to safety while providing my own ass for them to ogle.

"Is it?" I said, taking the mic. "Is it really the most wonderful time of year when anyone can slap on a beard and cater to his own monstrous jolliness? So appropriate that Santa lives where he does, because so many of you Santas live and die by your own poles. Did you really need another excuse to act like drunken jerks? Did you have to create one more white-male myth where it's the old white guy judging everyone and dispensing all the gifts? We all know who really buys those gifts, and that is a pretty strong argument for it being Mother Christmas in charge, no? Also, didn't you get the memo that you're supposed to be aiming for *nice*, not *naughty*? I'm not supposed to be able to smell the Christmas spirit on your breath, you jolly Saint Nickheads."

"Get off the stage!" one of the Santas hollered.

"No, sir." I turned to the more earnest carolers. "I think the stage should belong to the people who want to sing, not the people who want to dick around. Can I get an amen?"

"Amen!" the carolers yelled. Except, since they were British, it came out sounding like, "Why, yes, I think so, amen."

The drunk Santas held fast, refusing to relinquish their positions.

"There's only one thing to do," I whispered to Lily. "You have to deploy 'Silent Night.'"

She looked at me blankly. I realized that, since she'd been oblivious to the simulated groping, it looked to her like I was randomly picking a fight with Santa(s).

"Okay, then," I said. And then, seeing no other way out of it, I began to sing. . . .

Silent night, holy night . . .

There were a few hiccups, but soon the earnest carolers

were with me. The carol-oke machine was off. It was just us, singing into the night.

All is calm, all is bright . . .

There are many wonderful things about "Silent Night." Somehow it calms everyone down like the divinest form of lullaby. Almost everyone knows the words, and because it's quiet, you feel less self-conscious singing along. It feels time-less, but it also links to all of the other times you've heard it in your life. And, in this particular case, it is a song that is impossible to be a raging jerk within. If you're not part of the harmony, you have to cede the stage. As we moved into the first verse, the drunk Santas were disarmed.

I put the mic down—"Silent Night" doesn't need any soloists. And as soon as I did, the earnest carolers gathered around me and Lily.

Sleep in heavenly peace.

Sleep in heavenly peace.

The crowd hushed. It felt like the entire city hushed. A few people turned on the flashlights on their phones and waved them in the air like lighters. Others waved lighters. The song was spinning its own magnificent constellations.

It would have been impossible to not be moved by it.

Lily, though, was more than moved. She was shaken. It was at that moment I realized she was, in fact, intoxicated by more than just the caroling. It wasn't that tears had formed in her eyes; no, she was completely sing-sobbing, or sob-singing. This is what can happen when a song creates such a caesura; in the calmest pause, other emotions can surface.

Especially if you've been drinking. The song unlocks the depths. The breath becomes the sob.

But we sang on, because the choir and the congregation were the same body right now, and that body was going to carry us to the final notes. The bad Santas had slunk away, and all that was left was the voices of the rest of us.

When it was over, there was a brief pause, the length of a good exhalation. Then there was a rousing cheer, and people started hugging and smiling. I hugged Lily close, but she would not stop crying.

"What is it?" I asked. "What's wrong?"

"I ruined Christmas," she said. "I ruined everybody's Christmas."

"No, you didn't," I assured her.

"My family hates me."

"No, they don't."

As we walked off the makeshift stage, Azra was waiting in the makeshift wings. Solo.

"What happened to your posh male accessory?" I asked. Then, seeing the expression on her face, I had to ask, "Has there been an Olivier twist?"

"Too soon," Lily mumbled to me.

"Too late," Azra said, followed by a sigh. "Olivier and I are no longer together."

"Oh," I said. "I didn't see that one coming."

"Well," Azra said, "neither did I."

"It's just so *sad*," Lily told me.

"How many has she had?" I asked Azra.

"Plenty," Azra replied. "It seemed like a good idea at the time."

"I'm fine," Lily said. "I can walk. I can do math in my head. Test me. Ask me the square root of something."

"The fact that you even know what a square root is bodes well," I observed.

"It's not like when I first met you," Lily said. "It doesn't hit me as hard. It just makes me a little"—here she paused to yawn—"sleepy."

"I guess you've built up something of a tolerance," I said.

Suddenly Lily made a retching noise. I couldn't tell whether it was a reaction to the liquor or to what I'd said.

"Hairball?" I inquired.

"That word!" Lily spat out. "*Tolerance*. How can it apply to both how I handle my drinking and how my family handles you?!"

I hoped the question was rhetorical, because it left me speechless.

Azra stepped in. "Her family has been texting incessantly. Telling her Christmas is canceled this year because she jetted off. Not fair, if you ask me."

"I should text them back!" Lily proclaimed, taking out her phone. "I really should!"

"No!" Azra and I said at the same time, both of us lunging for the phone. Lily snapped it away from us . . . then put it back in her pocket.

"Okay okay okay," she said. "Now what?"

"I think we should call it a night," I said. It wasn't long

past nine, but I knew that if Lily had been up all day, the jet lag would be having something to say on top of the blood-alcohol level.

Azra nodded. "Her bags are already at Claridge's."

I was very relieved to hear I wouldn't have to deal with Mark.

"Also," Azra added, "you should know that your texts to her aren't coming through. You'll need to get your mobiles sorted out. Or maybe it was just a glitch. See what happens when you're on wifi."

"Thanks for the tip," I said. "And thanks for tipping us off about where you were. I am sorry to hear about you and Olivier. Even if the two of you together were pretty—"

"Insufferable?"

"Well, yeah. But you alone. You're—"

"Sufferable?"

Probably for the first time ever, Azra had made me smile. "Exactly."

And, lo and behold, I had made her smile back. "I'm going to call my family's driver and have him take you to Claridge's. I'm going to meet up with some people a short walk away, so I won't need him for a bit."

"I mean, if you have an extra driver just sitting around . . . ," I said.

"Thank you," Lily chimed in.

"Yeah, that too."

Azra said to call her tomorrow and that hopefully we could make more plans. Then she walked us to the street and introduced us to her driver, who was wearing a suit and cap like he'd just come from being an extra in an episode of *The Crown*. He did not question who we were or why he had to take us. He barely gave us any expression at all.

Once we were ensconced in the back of the car, I could tell there was a string of sorrys about to unfurl from Lily's lips.

"I'm sorry, too," I said before she could get any of her own out. "Bygones?"

Lily thought about it for a moment, then rested her head on my shoulder.

"Bygones," she murmured.

In less than a minute, she was asleep.

I had to wake her when we got to the hotel.

"Are we there?" she asked, opening her eyes.

"Yes," I said, wondering if she had any idea where *there* was.

This wondering was soon dismissed, because when Lily stepped out of the car, she did so as if she was returning home. She thanked the driver with such sweet gratitude that he almost melted into an expression. Then she said hello to the doormen like she'd been coming here for years.

When we got inside the lobby, I started to wonder if I was the one dreaming, and if we'd stepped back into the Jazz Age. There were chandeliers aplenty, and black-and-white tile floors that just begged for a big tap-dance number to play across them. A huge Christmas tree made of crystals and light presided by a grand staircase. It was, in the word of Cole Porter, a swellegant place to be.

"Not bad, huh?" Lily asked, a glint in her eye.

"Wow," I admitted.

As we rode the elevator up to our floor, I could see Lily's burst of energy start to dissipate. She took off her coat, and by the time we were walking to our room, she was practically dragging it on the ground.

"Here," I said, picking it up. "Allow me."

It took another minute for her to find the room key and open the door.

The room itself was as deco as the lobby, on a much smaller scale. A king-size bed was the sovereign of the space.

"I want to start kissing you," Lily said with a yawn, "but I'm just"—another yawn—"so"—yawn—"*tired*."

"One now, many more later?" I offered.

She nodded. We kissed. And as she pulled away, she declared, "I think I want to sleep in that robe."

Before I could ask, "What robe?" she had disengaged a very plush robe from the closet and stepped into the bathroom. I noticed she hadn't unpacked, then went and checked out the view from the window, over nighttime Mayfair.

When Lily returned from the bathroom, she was indeed only wearing the robe. Which would have been sorely enticing in other circumstances, but now every ounce of her being was radiating sleepiness.

She came over to me, kissed me on the cheek, then kept walking and collapsed onto the bed.

Once again, she was asleep within a minute. First gently, and then with a snoring crescendo.

I turned off the lights, kicked off my shoes, and stepped into the bathroom. Lily's clothes were sprawled over the floor, left wherever she'd dropped them.

I sent a text to Gem.

Staying over at Claridge's with Lily. See you tomorrow.

About two seconds after I hit Send, Gem called.

"Hello?" I answered.

"Just making sure that the only thing you're under the influence of is love, dear," Gem said.

"Nothing but love, I assure you."

"Okay, then. As long as I get to see you tomorrow at some point, and as long as I get to spend time with Lily as well. It's very strange—I'd gotten quite used to solitary Christmases, but now that you're here . . . I guess it changes things, doesn't it? So yes. I have some things to do during the day, but maybe an early supper? You don't have to answer now. In the meantime, I'm going to give Katarina a call. She's a concierge at Claridge's. We go way back—arguably, her meddling caused me to lose out on a date with Prince Charles. So she owes me. I'll make sure you have provisions within ten minutes. There will be a knock on the door."

Before I could tell her that wasn't necessary, she was signing off and wishing me a good night. Ten minutes later there was a soft knock on the door; I answered and found a bellhop, who offered me a neatly folded pair of silk pajamas and a toiletry kit. I thanked her, then went into the bathroom to change, leaving my clothes alongside Lily's.

I had never understood silk pajamas conceptually before. Now I understood them a little more. Whereas flannel felt like a warm blanket, this felt like gliding within gossamer sheets.

When I got into bed, Lily shifted, her snores abating, at least momentarily.

"Hey, you," she said.

I cuddled in, and together we fell into a sound, luxurious sleep.

thirteen

LiLY

December 23rd

"Are you hungover?" Dash asked me as I squinted at the morning light streaming in through the windows whose curtains he'd just opened. "You look blinded."

"I'm blinded by your pajamas!"

He grasped the hem of his pajama top. "You don't like them?"

"I LOVE them!" I said. "I just never imagined you in purple silk pajamas. You're like a magnificent Prince dreamscape. Where did you get them?"

"The concierge sent them up for me. She's a friend of Gem's."

"I'd love to have heard that conversation last night between your grandmother and the concierge about your sleep needs, because I'm pretty sure you're wearing ladies' pajamas."

"If I'd known how comfortable they were, I'd have started wearing ladies' pajamas years ago."

"Can I take a photo of you?" Honestly, he'd never looked hotter to me.

"Yes. But don't send it to Langston. It'll only give him ammunition in his suspicions about my sexual orientation."

"The pajamas won't do that. Your love of Cate Blanchett and Carly Rae Jepsen does." Dash laughed. I grabbed my phone from the nightstand and snapped a photo of him. I was already thinking about how to photoshop it into some kind of sexy Valentine's Day card that I'd send to myself. "Please, come closer so I can run my hands across that purple silk."

With no warning, he jumped back into bed, causing me to go flying from his bounce. My head banged against the bed's headboard. "Now I might have a hangover," I said. "But it's a happy headache. I'm so happy you're here."

He came in for a kiss, which I eagerly delivered to him. Then I pulled back. "I'm sorry about yesterday."

"You don't need to be sorry. I always enjoy your caroling, even drunk."

"Not about that. I'm sorry for jumping ship when I did."

"Oh, yes, you should be sorry about that. Apology accepted. What was that all about, anyway?"

I told him about feeling overwhelmed after announcing to my family that I had no intention to go to Barnard next year. Dash said, "That's big. When you told me about the dog school in Twickenham, I realized you were seriously reconsidering Barnard, but I didn't know you'd made a definitive decision. How'd it go over?"

"Not well." I turned on the wifi on my phone to show him the angry texts from my mother. And of course, once the wifi was on, I started receiving texts from Dash from after I'd gotten off the boat yesterday, and the ones I'd been trying to send him afterward started going through. "Hey, our phones are finally talking to each other. The texts I tried sending you yesterday kept bouncing back."

Dash took my phone from my hand and tossed it to the floor. "Let's forget about our phones today. About our families. About—"

"Yes!" I beckoned him toward me for what I really wanted to focus on today. Kissing him.

But—

Ring.

It was the doorbell to the hotel room. It sounded so politely British, not like an aggressive New York doorbell's *RING RING RIIIIIIIING.* "Did you call for something?" I asked Dash, who shook his head.

He got up and answered the door. "Compliments of the concierge, sir," said a uniformed waiter outside in the hall. Dash opened the door to him. The waiter carted in a silver tray. "Where would you like it?"

"On the desk, I guess?" said Dash. "What is it?"

"Morning coffee and pastries." The waiter placed the tray

on the desk alongside a white pot that smelled like just the delicious antidote to my slight hangover.

Dash signed for the delivery, and the waiter left.

"Coffee?" Dash asked me.

"Yes, please!" He poured me a coffee. As he delivered it to me in his purple pajamas, I added, "Then I want to devour you."

But coffee first. I sat up in bed, leaning against the headboard, and Dash sat alongside me. We each took our first sips. It was perfection—strong, smooth, and not at all bitter.

Dash said, "I have to admit I was wrong about your hotel choice. I thought it was a terrible idea to spend so much money, but now that I've stayed here, I appreciate you being a dog-walking mogul who can spring for it."

"Thank you. And agreed!"

"I used to dismiss my mother when she talked about nonsense like the thread count of sheets, but I get it now. These sheets are amazing."

"Right? So soft and yet crisp at the same time. I thought I was fancy when my mom bought me the most expensive sheets at Target. They're sandpaper in comparison to Claridge's sheets."

"The marble bathroom!" Dash said.

"The fresh flowers on the nightstand!"

"This coffee is so good! All other hotels are officially dead to me."

"We should come here for our honeymoon," I joked.

"You're really going to have to step up your dog crafts business, then," Dash teased. "I'll expect the finest honeymoon suite. I doubt my future English literature degree will land me the job to finance a Claridge's honeymoon."

"This room even smells good!" I said.

"I know! I thought it was just my imagination. It smells like lavender and mint and clotted-cream scones. Speaking of which . . ."

Dash got up and returned to the bed with the tray. He took the silver dome off it, revealing an assortment of freshly baked scones next to a bowl of clotted cream and tiny jars of jam. He spread some clotted cream and raspberry jam (my favorite—I loved that he didn't need to ask) onto one and handed it to me. I took a bite, then sighed. "Best. Breakfast. Ever."

"We can never leave."

"Please let's never leave." I took another bite. "Do you think Boris could come live here with us?"

Dash shook his head. "It was such a nice fantasy, Lily. Don't ruin it. These sheets were probably woven by Egyptian cotton fairies. Boris would destroy them within seconds."

My sweet Boris! I ached from missing him. But the coffee had removed the speck of headache, and all the deliciousness had given me a moment of clarity. "I know what I want to do," I told Dash.

"Do you mean, like, which scone you want next, or with your life?"

"I want the lemon-glazed scone next. But I meant with my life. I want to be a dogpreneur."

"Is that actually a thing?"

"Of course it is. I want to be with dogs, train dogs, and design dog crafts. I want to make a business out of dogs. A serious business. Not just a 'gap-year distraction,' as my mother calls it. I don't see why that should be a disappointment as a life's calling."

"I never said it was."

"I know. My parents will. I guess I'm rehearsing what I'm going to say to them."

"Would you like some advice?"

"Generally, no. But from you and your magnificent purple-pajama'd self, yes."

"The talk with your parents will go better if you have an alternative to Barnard in mind."

"I just told you what the alternative is. I want to be a dogpreneur."

"Lily." Dash set aside his coffee and looked at me intently. "I say this with all the love I have for you in my heart. Please tell me you want more from your life than just being around dogs."

I was glad I was having this practice talk with Dash, because I knew what he'd just said was exactly the argument my parents would make. Somehow, if they said it, I knew I'd react angrily and defensively. But hearing it from Dash made me consider it reasonably.

I said, "Of course I want more from my life. I'd like to be involved in volunteer rescue work for all animals, not just dogs. I'd like to work with the elderly—maybe by bringing therapy animals to visit with them. And I really enjoy crafting clothes and accessories. For dogs and humans. I would love to get better at sketching and sewing—"

"Have you ever considered FIT?" Dash asked me.

"No. Why?"

"Where's your laptop?"

"In my backpack."

Dash retrieved my laptop and returned to the bed. He navigated to the website for the Fashion Institute of Technology in Manhattan. We perused its course selections. There were so many subjects I was actually interested in! (Sorry, Barnard.) Accessories design. Entrepreneurship. Illustration. Packaging design. Textile development and marketing. TOY DESIGN!

"I had no idea I could feel so excited about going to college," I said. "I want to take all those courses!"

Dash said, "The application deadline is a week away. You could get it done in time."

"But you're supposed to submit a portfolio, too. I can't—"

"You have enough photos from the crafts you sell on Instagram to use as a portfolio. You know I find chasing social media likes to be disingenuous, but in this case, I'd say all the likes on your photos are testament to how good your work is."

"You really think I should apply to FIT?" I didn't need his answer. I already knew I wanted to do it.

"I do. It seems like a much better *fit* for you." He waited for me to laugh at his pun. I didn't. He could do so much better than low-level dad jokes. "And I think turning down Barnard would go down a lot better with your parents if you had an alternative education plan in mind, and not just a desire to be a dogpreneur." He paused. "I feel ridiculous when I say that word."

"I love you when you're ridiculous." I programmed my laptop to stream a playlist courtesy of the original Purple One. It started exactly where I planned to spend the rest of the morning—with the song "Kiss."

"This is kinkier than I expected," Dash whispered into my ear.

"I know!" I whispered back. "It's so perfect in its awfulness."

We were at the matinee performance of *Happy Chrimbo, Dick Whittington*, tickets for which we'd been given the previous day by the actor on *The Thames of Our Lives*.

I knew the British were famous for the theater. That guy Shakespeare, he was pretty good. Their movie actors who came from the theater are the best of the best, like those *X-Men* old guys, and my favorite, Helen Mirren, the voice of the Queen in my favorite movie last Christmas, *Corgi & Bess*. Plus, two words: Idris Elba.

But this pantomime showcased an over-the-top acting style that seemed like a very distant cousin to the grand

West End theater tradition. It was strictly high camp, with cross-dressing actors wearing outrageous costumes and a sadly sparse audience that behaved exactly the opposite of how I'd expect a proper British audience to respond. They yelled things like "Sod off!" when a villain appeared, and "He's behind you!" to warn the good guy, Dick Whittington, when the villain approached. They hooted and hollered when Dick Whittington finally got his Chrimbo (British slang for *Christmas*) wish fulfilled: The King Rat was destroyed by London's wiliest cat (played by a D-list reality-TV star from a British show called *Telly Me Everything, Mate*).

It was like going to an audience sing-along of *Moulin Rouge!*, but more bonkers, more glitter, more confetti, and *definitely* more beer being drunk by attendees than I'd ever seen, well, ever.

"This was totally worth leaving Claridge's," I whispered to Dash.

"Was it?" he whispered back.

"Shush!" said an intoxicated audience member behind us who, minutes earlier, had shouted "Telly me everything!" to the corpulent, blustering actor playing Alice Fitzwarren, Dick Whittington's wife.

Dash ignored the shushing, and the request to turn off cell phones. He showed me a message on his phone. "We're being summoned back to Claridge's for afternoon tea," he said, not bothering to whisper anymore.

"By who?"

"I don't know. Katarina just said we needed to be back by half three."

"I don't know what 'half three' means."

"Three-thirty!" the audience member behind us bellowed. "Go on, then. We're trying to enjoy the show."

"Glad to oblige," said Dash. He got up, and so did I.

Once outside, I asked Dash, "How relieved are you?"

"So relieved."

"I loved it," I admitted. Between burning letters to that patron saint of patriarchy, Father Christmas, the Hyde Park Winter Wonderland, and now the Christmas "panto," I was seriously enamored of British holiday merrymaking. Big fan.

"Have you ever been to a proper British afternoon tea?" Dash asked me.

"No."

"Trust me, you'll love it more."

Returning to Claridge's that afternoon gave me my first opportunity to really appreciate the spectacle of the Art Deco hotel. It was a redbrick building decorated with flags billowing above its entrance; inside its main foyer was a dazzling display of crystal chandeliers, checkerboard tiles, paneled walls, antique gilt mirrors, and flower arrangements taller than me. Piano music and the sound of teaspoon clinks drifted through the elegant lobby.

Dash and I found the host at the tearoom and gave him

our names. "Right this way, sir," said the host. He led us away from the foyer, which almost made me want to cry until I saw the next room, which was our destination. "Your reservation is in the Reading Room, and the first member of your party is already seated."

I didn't need to ask who our mystery tea companion was, because I knew by the faint aroma of Chanel No. 19 ("No. 5 is so boring") wafting from the velvet-upholstered banquette where the host directed us.

Mrs. Basil E. stood up when she saw us. She nodded to the host. "Thank you, Geoffrey."

He bowed to her before leaving. "Lovely to have you here again, madam."

Mrs. Basil E. placed a kiss on my cheek and a pat on Dash's shoulder. "You're late," she told us as she returned to her seat.

"It's three-forty," Dash said. "We only got your invitation an hour ago."

"Punctuality is a virtue," she said.

"So is fair warning of an ambush," said Dash.

Mrs. Basil E. laughed. "You are a delight, in your inimitably snarly way."

"Thank you," said Dash. "Vice versa."

My great-aunt was my one family member who not just *tolerated* Dash, but actually enjoyed him. And vice versa.

"What are you doing here?" I asked.

"I was jealous when I heard you'd skipped town to come here. So I decided to join you."

"Any other reason?" Dash asked.

Mrs. Basil E. said, "There's a rumor going around that Lily is dropping out of college."

"I knew it," said Dash, affirmed once again in his conviction of my family's overcontrolling nature.

"I never *started* college!" I said.

Dash said, "And we may have resolved the issue. Perhaps the problem was not that Lily was not in college, but that she chose the wrong one to attend . . . next year, not this year, by the way."

Mrs. Basil E. fixed her gaze on me. "My mother, your great-grandmother, went to Barnard! I went to Barnard! Your grandmother went to Barnard. How do you think she met Grandpa? Because I introduced them. When we were *at Barnard*."

Dash said, "Am I the only one who realizes the complete absurdity of Lily planning her future based on that logic?"

"Being a legacy doesn't mean I should go there," I said.

"Then why did you apply?" Mrs. Basil E. asked.

"Because it was near Grandpa's home and because everyone else besides me seemed confident it was where I belonged."

"And an exceptional amount of family pressure," Dash added.

"Those are all good reasons," said Mrs. Basil E.

Dash offered, "Lily's thinking about applying to FIT to study design and entrepreneurship."

Mrs. Basil E. nodded. "Not a bad option, actually. But Barnard. No one in our family has ever gone to FIT."

Dash's hand made the motion of an airplane. He said, "This family. Once again, logic flies away."

Then it occurred to me: "Didn't you drop out of Barnard?" I asked Mrs. Basil E.

"Indeed. I only lasted a year."

"Why'd you drop out?" Dash asked.

She smiled. "His name was Henri. I met him when I did nude modeling for a figure-drawing program at Pratt. We took off to wander Europe for a year—maybe it was two?—afterward. Glorious time of my life."

I didn't say aloud what I was thinking but I psychically telegraphed it to Dash: *Hypocrite!* His lips upturned slightly into one of his rare smiles, which make me swoon. I patted his knee under the table. To Mrs. Basil E., I said, "So you didn't regret dropping out?"

"God, no."

"Then why shouldn't Lily also exercise her right not to go?" Dash asked Mrs. Basil E.

To me, she said, "You may, I suppose. But you need *purpose* if you opt out. Dogs are not enough. I may be swayed by the idea of FIT, but I'll need to think on it." She began inspecting the afternoon tea menu. "Where are you staying, by the way? With Mark and his terrible Ikea couch collection? I'd really hoped marriage would improve his design aesthetic."

"I'm staying at Claridge's," I said. "I thought that's why you summoned us here."

She laughed, then saw that I was serious. "I summoned you here because it's where *I'm* staying. I gave the concierge your names and told her to send you the invitation. I didn't realize you were already here."

"You telling me about it is why I always wanted to stay here!" I said.

"Who paid for it?" she asked.

"*I* paid for it."

"With what money?"

"My own! I sold a lot more dog crafts than I expected, and I got a big windfall from Christmas tips from my clients."

"You couldn't have possibly earned enough to pay for this hotel at peak holiday rates."

"I did. I paid for it mostly using the bonus from one very wealthy and grateful dog-walking client who said I added years of life to his arthritic dog. That dog never used to want to leave the apartment and now she's chasing pigeons in Tompkins Square Park again like a puppy. Also, he bought a ton of the dog sweaters I designed."

"You must be very good at what you do," said Mrs. Basil E.

"I am," I said, as Dash said, "She is."

"That's an admirable purpose," Mrs. Basil E. said. "Perhaps you do have a future in it that does not require a Barnard education." The waiter came by to take our orders. "Shall I order for us?"

Dash and I both nodded. She'd order for us regardless.

Mrs. Basil E. told the waiter, "We'll have the Claridge's Blend for my Oxford friend here, who I recall is partial to English breakfast teas. And the vegetarian sandwich options for my niece, who insists on compassion for animals and the earth, despite how delicious bacon is."

My love affair with England deepened when the tea service started. It wasn't just the beauty of the porcelain and the delicious aroma coming from the teapot. It was the *precision* with which the waiter poured the tea into our cups, like a master circus performer walking a tightrope with complete focus and yet complete ease. It almost didn't matter how the tea tasted; I was so impressed by the artful dome of the pour, ending with our cups filled to exactly the right proportion, with no splash whatsoever. The pour alone was its own kind of art.

"Do you take milk with your tea?" Mrs. Basil E. asked Dash.

"There's no need to offend me," said Dash.

"Good man," said Mrs. Basil E. approvingly.

Dash took his first sip, requiring no milk or sugar additions, as I did for my tea. After he swallowed, he said, "That's the best tea I've ever tasted."

I felt the same about the assortment of sandwiches that accompanied the tea. English cucumber with lemon and watercress cream on white bread. Peppered goat cheese with pumpkin and sage. The delicate sandwiches were served on a three-tiered china stand that I wanted to cover in a napkin before I left and steal back to America. (*Shoplifters of the world unite*, as that Morrissey once crooned. *Don't listen to that rapscallion, Lily*, I reminded myself.) "Whoever thought up these sandwiches should be knighted by the Queen," I said.

Mrs. Basil E. said, "I'm glad you approve, although I'm appalled by the way you drink your tea, Lily. Now, Dashiell. Tell me about Oxford. Is it everything you'd hoped?"

"I like England very much," said Dash. "Not so sure about Oxford."

"Why is that?" she asked him.

"There's the fantasy and there's the reality. I coasted on the fantasy since I was a kid. The reality as an adult is disappointing. Like, I always knew I wanted to study English literature. But that's *all* I study there. I might have liked to also study psychology, and Asian history, and African art, and South American magical realism. I feel more restricted than I anticipated."

"So perhaps it's not Oxford that's the problem," said Mrs. Basil E. "It's that the British university system is not a match for you. Perhaps it's *you* who should take a gap year, to figure out exactly what it is you'd like to study, and where."

"I miss New York," Dash admitted.

"Of course you do," she said.

"I like it here!" I chimed in. "I got into a dog school just outside of London. So that's also an option I'm considering."

Mrs. Basil E. set her raisin scone back down on her plate

and glared at me. "I have only just gotten used to the idea that you won't attend Barnard. I will not hear of you moving here to go to dog school. That's preposterous. YOU ARE A NEW YORKER. England is a dalliance. Not the real love affair." She took a sip of her tea and turned to Dash. "The same goes for you." Then: "Did I tell you Gerta has finally retired to Scottsdale, Arizona?"

"What does Gerta have to do with where Dash and I belong?" I asked her, confused. Gerta was my great-aunt's longtime housekeeper, who'd been living for the last year in a very dark, very small basement apartment in Mrs. Basil E.'s town house and had never once been the subject of our meal conversations.

"She's gone to live with her sister and to reunite with the sun. So here is what I think." Mrs. Basil E. took one of my hands, and one of Dash's hands, and placed our hands together. "The solution is clear. I will deny it was my suggestion to your respective parents, of course. But I think you two should move into the basement apartment. Find your purpose there, together."

I almost spat my tea out of my mouth but would never sully the sanctity of Claridge's Reading Room with my American buffoonery, so I didn't.

Dash sweetly squeezed my hand but told my great-aunt, "You know how much I love your niece. But I don't think Lily and I are in any position at this stage of our lives to talk about moving in together."

"Agreed," I said. Was she *insane*?

Mrs. Basil E. said, "I'm not talking about just being room-mates of convenience because Lily's great-aunt owns a choice piece of real estate. I'm saying you two should get married. Elope!"

My poor, beloved great-aunt. She'd indeed gone insane.

fourteen

DASH

December 23rd

"What are you *talking about?*" Lily yelled, surprised and outraged.

I was calmer . . . because I know a bluff when I see one.

"She's not serious," I assured Lily. "I'm sure there's a psychological term for what she's doing . . . but I don't know it, since I wasn't allowed to take a psych course. In any case, she's saying these things so we'll go on the record as not wanting them. We establish that we don't want to run off together. Then we establish that we don't need to live together, or even be in the same city in order to be a couple. Which leads to the conclusion . . ." I turned to Mrs. Basil E. "It's your line."

Mrs. Basil E. sighed. "You might as well go to Barnard."

"Are you kidding me?" Lily asked.

I continued to talk to her great-aunt. "I hope you don't

mind me saying so, Mrs. Basil E., but your files are *seriously* mixed up right now."

Mrs. Basil E. dropped the subject then, but it was hard for us to pick any other subject back up. We sipped and savored in silence until the plates were cleared and the tiered tower of teatime delicacies was returned to the kitchen, no doubt to be polished by house elves.

I looked at my watch.

"We should probably get going," I said. "My grandmother will be waiting for us. Thank you for the tea, if not the sympathy."

As we stood up to leave, Mrs. Basil E. said, "Lily, I have some evening engagements, but I should be back in my room by ten o'clock. I expect you to join me for a nightcap. *Alone.*"

"Okay," Lily said quietly.

"Don't act like it's a walk to the gallows," Mrs. Basil E. chided.

"I'll be sure we've married and taken out a mortgage on a dream home by the time you next see her," I said.

I was trying to draw some of Mrs. Basil E.'s withering glances my way, and in this I was highly successful.

"You can stop being so irascible," she said to me. "You are threatening to bring out the harm that lies within your charm. I promise you, I have not crossed the Atlantic just for the sake of pithy banter. You are both at very important crossroads, and I fear you are going to take the wrong paths."

"Right now our only path is to the nearest Tube station," I told her.

"I'll see you later," Lily added, hugging her great-aunt good-bye.

Lily and I didn't say anything to each other until we were out of the hotel; it was not unreasonable to think Mrs. Basil E. would have spies throughout the lobby, alert to any sarcasm on my part, and any regret on Lily's. It was only as we were walking to the Tube that I let out a "What just happened?!" and Lily released an "I have no idea!"

All the talk of elopement put Carly Rae Jepsen's "Run Away with Me" in my head. I shared this fact with Lily as we stepped on the kilometer-long escalator to get to the heart of the Underground.

"I really wasn't expecting those words to come out of her mouth," Lily said. "Ever."

"Somehow I don't think that's the remedy your parents would have wanted her to propose," I said. "Even if it was just to steer you back toward Barnard."

"I'm not going to Barnard."

"I know."

"Thank you."

She was on the step above me on the escalator, so we were practically the same height. I leaned in and kissed her.

"What was that for?" she asked.

"For not going to Barnard."

As the escalator neared the end of its run, we could hear a busker take up the opening strains of Joni Mitchell's "River," a maudlin holiday song that was one of Lily's favorites. But then, after the opening strains, something remarkable happened—the busker changed the tune so that she was using Joni's overture to lead to a piano version of . . . "Run Away with Me."

"No way," I said.

The busker looked strangely like Carly Rae Jepsen. But it couldn't be. Could it?

I was not the only person curious and enchanted. Others were stopping to sway to the song.

"One sec," I told Lily. "I have to do this."

And Lily smiled and said, "I know."

Of course she knew. I'd told her before of my vow: If I ever heard a busker who happened to be playing the song playing in my head, I would empty all the cash in my wallet into their guitar case.

I'd always assumed I'd get snagged by a Beatles song. It meant more that it was Carly Rae Jepsen.

As the busker sang, I took out my wallet, removed all the bills, and put them in a tinsel-decorated cookie tin that the busker was using in lieu of a guitar case. Then, for good measure, I emptied out all my change.

The busker looked a mix of confused and appreciative as she plunged into the chorus—

Hey, run away with me
Run away with me. . . .

As commuters pushed around us, I spun Lily around. A few other couples and singles joined in, singing along when the next chorus graced us.

Lily grabbed my hand and pulled me away so the song

could be the wind behind our back as we made our way forward. We were both grinning when we got onto the train, and we weren't the only ones.

By the time we got to the stop near Gem's flat, normalcy had reasserted itself.

"I'm nervous," Lily admitted as we walked through Waterloo. "I don't think I made the best first impression."

"Trust me," I said. "You have nothing to worry about."

When we got to the door, Lily went to knock, and I gently pointed out that I had a key. I let us in, then called out to Gem when we were in the foyer. The flat smelled like cinnamon and vanilla. A Tom Jones Christmas album was playing over the speakers.

Gem came out of the kitchen wearing an apron—not her usual look.

"There you are!" she said, hugging me and then hugging Lily. "I've been busy making your great-great-grandmother's Christmas cake. Which is really just a glorified coffee cake . . . but it's still tradition."

"I had no idea Dash had a family Christmas cake," Lily said.

"Neither did I!" I admitted.

This surprised Gem. At least at first. "Did your father never—no, I imagine he didn't. Well, I'll have to give you the recipe. We'll just say it skipped a generation."

"It smells wonderful," Lily said.

"Thank you, dear. I do enjoy throwing a dinner party.

During the lean years, by which I mean the years of nouvelle cuisine, people always loved coming here because they knew they'd get to eat heartily. Never underestimate the power of a well-dressed coffee cake to make even Londoners happy. Now, Dash, give her a tour and settle into your room for a bit. Dinner will be ready in an hour or so. Be sure to dress for it."

"Any particular dress code?" I asked.

"Oh, you'll see," Gem answered, without further explanation.

She went back into the kitchen, and I commenced the tour. When we poked our heads into the dining room, I discovered that Gem had transformed it into a holiday wonderland, complete with a centerpiece that was a Christmas tree made entirely of flowers.

"None of this was here twenty-four hours ago," I told Lily, who was utterly delighted by it. I called out to the kitchen, "Where did you get all this?"

"My friends at Liberty were very appreciative of my help!" Gem called back.

Lily lifted one of the floral cloth napkins from one of the place settings. "Nice friends to have," she observed.

I took in the whole sight. "I'll say."

After showing her more of the ground floor, I took her up to my room.

"Welcome to my home away from my home away from home," I told her.

"Books, books, more books, some clothes, a few photos . . . looks a lot like your home to me," she said.

"Plus an Advent calendar," I pointed out.

"Yes, I noticed."

She walked over to the closet, where two Liberty garment bags were dangling on the door.

"What are these?" Lily asked.

"I have no idea," I answered.

One of them had Lily's name on it. The other had my name on it.

Lily unzipped hers first, unveiling a fabulous frock.

"This is . . . wow" was her reaction.

I found a dapper suit inside my bag, a little less elaborate than the one I'd worn to Daunt, but still rather extravagant.

"I must say, I like her friends at Liberty," I commented.

Lily hung the dress back where it had been on the door. Then she sat on my bed and looked at me earnestly.

"What are we going to do, Dash?" she asked.

And I understood: A lot had been thrown at us in the past couple of days. This was our first sober pause.

I hung my suit beside her dress.

I knew she was asking the question about our lives, but I decided to answer about our next hour instead.

"Well," I told her, "I think we'll be taking off some clothing, and then putting on different clothing. Perhaps with some activity in between. How does that sound?"

"It doesn't sound like a future," she said. "But it definitely sounds like a plan."

An hour later, when Gem called us down for dinner, we were just a few buttons short of being ready.

Amy Winehouse was sounding winedrunk in the speakers as we settled in—at least until Gem mentioned Nick Drake and saw that neither Lily nor I knew who that was. The record player soon fell into a bucolic groove that seemed to fit the December evening perfectly.

Gem asked about our day, and we gave her some of the better details. Our recounting of the pantomime spurred her to tell us about the time she worked with Monty Python on a holiday special that the BBC had refused to air . . . which then became a story about the time Maggie Smith, Angela Lansbury, and Gem had broken into a studio in order to record a ribald version of "You're the Top" for Richard Burton's birthday.

"You must understand, he wasn't with Liz at the time," Gem assured us.

We nodded as if we understood.

"But enough about me," Gem said. "We left off at the pantomime. Tell me about the rest of your day."

I wasn't sure whether Lily would want to talk about Mrs. Basil E.'s surprise visit and the way she turned into a Tearex upon Lily's resistance to the collegial path. But Lily told the whole story, using phrases like *sneak attack* and *complete disregard for what I want* and *they just don't understand.* She finished by sharing Mrs. Basil E.'s final words about going down the wrong path.

"Presumably that's the path away from Barnard?" Gem asked.

"I think it's safe to assume that," Lily replied.

"Okay, then," Gem said, putting down her wineglass before she'd taken another sip. "I have a question for both of you. I'm asking you because, frankly, nobody ever asked it of me when I was your age. And then I made the same mistake and didn't ask it of my son when the time came, because I was too angry at him and at the world to notice that it needed to be asked. Lily, I know I'm a stranger to you, and Dash, I know that even though I am less than a stranger to you, we also haven't truly known each other long enough for me to be invested one way or the other in the answer. So, that said, let me ask. . . . If I were to ask you what you want do to with your life, going forward—what would your heart answer?"

Lily didn't hesitate. "I want to work with dogs. Not just because I'm good at it. But because I'm good for them. I love doing it, and I also know it helps in some way."

"Excellent," Gem said. "Now, Dash—how about you?"

My answer was *I don't know*. But I wasn't satisfied by that answer. I felt there was another answer underneath. The answer, in Gem's words, that my heart would give.

"I want to work with books," I said. "That's what I want to do. Like Lily wants to work with dogs. I want to work with books. My future is books."

It felt so presumptuous to say it out loud.

But it also felt right.

Lily and Gem must have sensed this. They were both nodding.

"Good," Gem said. "Now we know."

Yes. Now we knew.

Gem surprised me by slapping the table—an American gesture amidst the British settings.

"Of course!" she said. Then she stood up. "I'll be back in a second. I need to make a phone call."

"So," Lily said, reaching across the table for my hand. "Books."

I took her hand. "Yes, books. And dogs."

She smiled at me. "Yes, dogs."

"You'll apply to that program at FIT."

"Let 'em try to stop me."

"They're just barking at the moon."

It felt like only a minute later that Gem was back at the table, looking very satisfied.

"Eleven o'clock tomorrow," she told me, sitting.

"What about it?" I asked.

"You'll be interviewing with St. John Blakemore."

"WHAT?!" I inquired. St. John Blakemore was perhaps the most famous literary editor in New York City.

"Blakey's here in town for the holidays, visiting his parents. I rang up and he said he'll see you at eleven."

"*Blakey?!*"

"Oh, I took care of him for a spot in the eighties when

his parents had to go underground for a bit because of the whole Rushdie thing. I've written a few things for him over the years."

"You have?"

"Oh, yes. Just some ghostwriting on a few memoirs. We who are celebrity-adjacent remember so much more than the celebrities themselves!"

"This is insane! I can't just have an interview with St. John Blakemore tomorrow."

"An interview for what?" Lily asked.

"Yeah," I said, turning to Gem. "An interview for what?"

"Whatever you make of it," she answered. "I'm sure you'll make quite an impression."

I felt like I was about to hyperventilate.

"Okay," I said. "This is happening."

"Meanwhile," Gem continued, "I'm afraid I don't know anyone commensurate in the canine world."

"That's all right," Lily said. "I think I have it figured out."

The rest of the meal consisted of me explaining to Lily who St. John Blakemore was, and of Gem skirting around all the nondisclosure agreements she'd signed to hint at whose memoirs she'd written.

Then came the Christmas cake, which was entirely delectable.

"Where have you been all my life?" I asked it.

"I'd love to know the same thing," Gem said.

"You said this was my great-great-grandmother's recipe. What was her name? What was she like?"

198

Gem smiled. "Her name was Anna, and when I was a kid, I called her Granna, because I was always throwing Grandma and Anna together. She loved to bake, but she didn't particularly love to eat. The joy came from seeing other people eat and enjoy whatever she'd made. We always told her she could open a bakery, but she didn't like the idea of charging people. She'd much rather show up at friends' doorways with some cookies she'd made, or a cake just out of the oven."

"Did my father know her?"

"A little. I'm not sure he'd remember. But she made him cookies in the shape of his favorite truck."

This made me laugh. "My father had a favorite truck?"

"Oh, yes!" Gem said. "Its name was Paul—Paul was the man at the toy store. Such a nice man! Anyway, Paul—the truck, not the man—is about the size of my hand. Your father was always losing him. I probably spent half his childhood looking between couch cushions or under the bed for where Paul had gone. Your father loved Paul so much. Even when he got older, he kept Paul by the side of his bed. If I ever moved it to a shelf, he'd always put Paul back there. Into high school, this was."

I found it very hard to imagine my father cherishing a toy truck like this.

"And where's Paul now?" I asked.

"Oh," Gem said. "I still have him. Up in my room. I guess he watches over me now."

Tears came into her eyes then, and her happiness wavered.

"Oh, Gem," I said, this time reaching over for her hand.

"It's all right," she said. "If I had to do it all over again, I'd definitely do it better. But we all say that, don't we? Or at least we should."

I looked over to Lily, who was also looking sad now.

"I miss my family," she said. "Being here with you two is great. But it also makes me miss my family. I wish there was a way to have Christmas in both places."

"But, Lily," Gem said. "There is. Of course there is."

"What do you mean?"

"There are only twenty-four hours in the day," Gem said. "Unless you're flying from east to west."

"Are you saying—?" I began.

"I'm saying let's celebrate Christmas here," Gem said. "And then let's celebrate it there. All of us."

"All of us?" I asked.

"Yes," Gem said purposefully. "It's time that we had a family Christmas, too. Even if we don't have much of a family left. It's about time we all got together."

I tried to wrap my mind around this. Lily was clearly doing the same.

"You don't have to answer right away," Gem hastened to add. "I have a dear friend at Virgin. I'll just drop her a line and see if we can reserve some last-minute seats."

"Okay," Lily said.

"Sounds right," I said.

"Everyone done? If so, let's clear. Lily, will you be staying with us tonight?"

"No, I—oh, goodness. What time is it?"

"Half past nine. Why?"

"Mrs. Basil E. will be waiting for me!"

Lily decided to do a quick change back into her old clothes, rather than try to explain to Mrs. Basil E. why she was wearing something new. Gem ordered her a car and invited her back tomorrow night for "a Christmas Eve surprise."

"Are you sure you don't want me to come with you?" I asked Lily right before she went. "I don't have to come for the nightcap; I could just be waiting in your room for after."

"No, I need to do this myself," Lily said. "I mean, by myself in the room with her. I know you'll be there, too, in spirit."

"We're in this together," I said, both a statement and a vow.

"Yes, we are," she said, kissing me good-bye.

"Good luck" was the last thing I said before she got in the car and headed out into the night.

fifteen

LiLY

December 23rd and December 24th

Dash must love his grandmother because that Christmas cake was so mediocre—dry, baked about three minutes too long, the frosting a bit lumpy because Gem probably didn't sift the powdered sugar. But it was exactly what made me finally love Gem. It had so much heart, just like her.

It was official. I totally called it wrong.

I loved Gem. I loved her house, I loved her music collection, I loved the bowls of Cadbury chocolates in every room, and I loved her warmth. Mostly, I loved how much she adored Dash. Not because she was biologically connected to him, but because she truly got him.

I was already thinking about what kind of dog she should get and how I could help make that connection. She should be paired with a breed whose qualities matched hers—friendly, alert, cheerful, courageous. *Pauses for Google matchmaking* I got it! A Westie would be ideal for Gem. They were going to be such great mates, whenever I found her future canine best friend.

I loved London, too. As the car from Gem's took me back to my hotel, I relished watching the city go by, bustling with energy like New York, but such a different energy. Where New York was raw and hurried, London was dignified and in no rush to please and impress, as if to tell visitors, *I've survived more than you could ever imagine. I do things my way—the proper way. Be dazzled by me or not; I'm not worried about your judgment.*

For the first time in my life at this time of year, Christmas was an afterthought. I savored the decorations and anticipation, of course, but the big day was secondary to my primary objective: enjoying the time in England with Dash. As much as I hoped he would return to New York permanently, I couldn't deny the charm of this place and of the family he'd found there. It was a good fit.

Because of that, I hadn't entirely ruled out the dog school in Twickenham, although I would definitely put in an application to FIT. A few days in December at the holidays was not enough time with Dash. I knew I was greedy, but I wanted the magic to last longer than a holiday interlude. I tried to focus on my present happiness and not speculate on my future loneliness, but I wasn't sure I could go back to how it was—me in New York and Dash at Oxford, an ocean and too many time zones between us.

I'd have to get back to work in New York ASAP, though,

because I'd blown through a significant amount of my savings to fly here, and my hotel splurge was completely irresponsible.

There was so much to see and do in London and I'd never get to it all before my flight home, but that was fine. Because, Claridge's. As I stepped out of the car and into the hotel lobby, I didn't regret my financially reckless whim at all. From the gracious staff who welcomed me back and remembered my name, to the jazz quartet playing in the foyer, to the rich sounds of lively conversations and smells of delicious food and drink, I knew I'd stepped into a fantasy that would soon end, but I'd enjoy it as long as I could. For sure I'd never be able to afford it again.

"You look too happy for a girl who's broken her family's heart," Mrs. Basil E. said to me as she greeted me in her hotel suite. I chose not to answer but instead inspected her "room." Holy moly! If hotel rooms were Broadway show tickets, then my single room was the back corner of the nosebleed seats, and Mrs. Basil E.'s palatial suite was private box seats just above the stage.

"Is this place even for real?" I asked her as I took a quick spin through the two-bedroom suite that had—wait for it—a GRAND PIANO in its living room. I sat down at the piano. "Is a grand piano a requirement for all your hotel bookings?"

Mrs. Basil E. said, "I prefer the Empress Eugenie Suite, which has no piano, but it was booked. I was only able to get this suite because of a last-minute cancellation."

"So this is a downgrade from your usual accommodations?"

"It's an even exchange. It's fine, but I prefer the décor in the Eugenie. The fabrics in this one are too modern for my tastes. But I'm hoping Mark will come over and use the piano."

"I forgot he played piano." It had been a welcome memory lapse. I imagined Mark playing what Grandpa called his Melancholy Piano Elegies—Mahler, Chopin, snooooze—on this suite's grand piano, and felt sad. *Poor piano,* I thought. *You deserve Ellington and Gershwin.* Then I remembered that was what my mother used to say in private at Mark's recitals and I remembered I was a schmuck.

Mrs. Basil E. said, "Hopefully this piano will be a good incentive for Mark to renew that talent. I didn't pay for all those years of his piano lessons with the expectation that he'd drop that interest for . . . books." She said that last word as if it was *diarrhea.*

"I thought you liked books."

"I love books. But piano playing can be shared by everyone. Particularly at my parties."

I stepped over to the couch. "I heard you canceled your big Christmas party this year."

"I heard you got Christmas canceled this year," she said. "What other choice did I have?"

"Touché," said I.

The doorbell rang. "That must be Adwin." She called to the door. "Please come in!"

"Who's Edwin?" I whispered. Who could possibly be calling on her so late in the evening?

We could hear the door opening in the foyer as Mrs. Basil E. quietly said to me, "It's Adwin, not Edwin. He's originally from Ghana and it was also his father's, grandfather's, and great-grandfather's name."

"Who *is* he?"

Adwin arrived in the room before Mrs. Basil E. could answer, but he needed no further explanation. He wore a butler's uniform and carted in a bottle of champagne on ice, along with champagne glasses and a tray of chocolate-covered strawberries.

He bowed to Mrs. Basil E. "Madam," he said formally.

"Thank you, Adwin.. Would you care to join us for an *après*?"

"Thank you kindly, madam. But my children are expecting Christmas presents, which means—"

"You'd better get started on your last-minute shopping?" Mrs. Basil E. asked him.

"Yes. Will you require anything further?"

"No, thank you. I look forward to seeing you tomorrow. And good luck with your shopping. I hear that Harry Potter is popular with the young ones."

"How old are your children?" I asked him.

"Twins. Age four," Adwin said.

"Too young for HP," I said. Then, as if I were Dash, the best of anyone I know at book recommendations, I added, "Captain Underpants is your man."

Adwin bowed to us again. "I'll take that under advisement. Good night." And he left the Grand Piano Suite.

Seriously, Lily, I said to myself. *You just said "Captain Underpants" to a fancy-pants Ghanaian-British butler. You are the definition of uncouth American!*

Aloud, I said to Mrs. Basil E., "Seriously . . . your room came with a *butler*?!"

"Isn't he charming? He speaks five languages, he's a fabulous pinochle player, *and* he makes the perfect martini. His husband's a lucky man." She stepped over to the silver cart with the champagne and strawberries on it. "I thought we should have some champagne."

"Because you're toasting my engagement or elopement or . . . WHAT WERE YOU THINKING EVEN SUGGESTING THAT TO ME AND DASH?"

"Don't raise your voice at me, young lady. I'm not toasting you. I'm disappointed in you. I thought this difficult conversation would go down better with some quality bubbly."

I gulped. My heart dropped. But she opened the champagne bottle with a New Year's Eve flourish and poured us each a glass.

"Why disappointed?" I asked, feeling very, very small. I took a sip of the champagne. It felt crisp in my mouth, with sturdy bubbles that tasted like happy, subtle fireworks going down my throat. It was actually a lovely precursor to being chewed out, as I suspected was about to happen.

"Deciding not to go to college and announcing that by email to someone other than your family is not the way to handle such an important decision."

"I know," I mumbled. "Sorry."

"Which brings us to the second disappointment. You should be apologizing to your mother, not to me. More importantly, your refusal to answer her calls and texts is cowardly, at best. Mean, at worst. You know better."

"I know," I repeated. "Sorry."

"You've upset my favorite niece and I don't appreciate it."

Hey, wait a minute. "I thought I was your favorite niece."

Mrs. Basil E. took a sip of her champagne, then said, "Your mother was my first favorite. Here, have a strawberry."

I'd kind of lost my appetite from being called out, but the strawberry was so perfectly red and so perfectly formed, and the chocolate so looked like it had been melted on by perfect Adwin himself, that it felt rude to decline. I took a bite. I was right. It would have been rude to decline.

"So what should I do?" I asked her.

"You know what to do. Apologize. Take responsibility for your actions. Because otherwise you know what is happening?" I shook my head. "They blame Dash."

"He had nothing to do with my decision!"

"But they don't know that, because you haven't explained it to them. In the absence of your honesty, and clarity, with your parents, the impression you've left by darting off to London at Christmas and then suddenly announcing you're not going to Barnard is that your boyfriend is your only real priority. They don't want you to blindly follow Dash."

"That's insulting."

"You have to understand they're operating from a place of fear, like Fox News viewers. Your parents married young—

too young. They've done fine, had their ups and downs like any other couple, but they're at an age where they're taking stock of their regrets and they're fearful of you repeating their mistakes. They worry you're holding yourself back by limiting yourself to one person so soon. They feel—and so do Grandpa and I—that you're too young to be in a serious relationship."

Had she already been drunk when we had afternoon tea earlier that day? "You're the one who suggested Dash and I get married!"

"I was trying to smoke you out. Gauge your true intentions toward Dash."

"So Dash was right!"

"He's too smart for his own good. But yes, he was right. So tell me, Lily. What are your intentions toward Dash? Do you intend to marry him?"

"How would I know? I mean, maybe, in the wayyyyy distant future. I have a lot of things I'd like to accomplish before then. Choosing not to go to Barnard has nothing to do with Dash and everything to do with me."

She nodded. "I'm glad to hear that."

"I'd like it if Dash and I lived closer. But it's not going to determine what I do or don't do in my immediate future." I took another sip of champagne. This stuff was good! And emboldening. "And another thing! I'm so sick of hearing how I'm too young to be in a serious relationship. If anything, you should be congratulating me for choosing someone like Dash, someone so smart, and kind—"

She waved her hand at me. "Enough of the Dash platitudes. We are all aware of his good qualities. But you're the baby of the family. We would have liked to see you experience more of the world independently, come into your own on your own. Perhaps you were ready. We weren't."

I thought of what my life might have been like in the last two years if I hadn't been involved with Dash, and I saw a life that might have been just as rewarding, certainly more overprotected . . . but so much less sweet. It wasn't that he'd filled some void in my life. He'd enriched it.

I didn't know what she wanted me to say. "I can't help loving him. What do you want me to do?"

"Be compassionate. I know you don't want to be the family baby and of course you shouldn't have to be. I *am* saying, be kinder to your parents and grandfather as you become more independent from them. Letting go is harder than you can imagine."

I could imagine. I let go of my boyfriend so he could follow his dream to Oxford and it had hurt like hell. But it was the right thing to do.

"I'll try," I said.

"They think you don't want to go to Barnard because you don't want the responsibility of helping care for Grandpa."

I'd had no idea they thought that. It was frustrating. "One has nothing to do with the other. Of course I want to be there for Grandpa."

"But this school you're considering in England?"

"It's a one-year program. I wouldn't be gone long. I'd come back home as much as I could."

"You wouldn't really move to England, would you?"

"If you mean *for Dash*, the answer is, maybe I would. But I wouldn't do it if I didn't have a very good reason to be here otherwise. One of the concentrations the dog school offers is learning how to work with therapy animals. That's a skill I'd like to bring back to Grandpa's nursing home."

"Interesting." Champagne sip. Strawberry bite. "I still don't approve. But you're going to do what you're going to do."

"And I'll still be your favorite niece, no matter what I choose."

She set her glass down. "You are excused. Go to your room and call my other favorite niece. Resolve this. Get Christmas un-canceled!"

"I'm sorry," I told Mom once I'd returned to my hotel room, which now seemed like a one-star travesty in comparison to Mrs. Basil E.'s Grand Piano Suite. But it was mine, and mine alone, and I'd earned it, and I loved my luxurious little hovel.

No phone filter could have helped how bad Mom looked—exhausted, like she hadn't slept in days, and puffy-faced, like there'd been a lot of crying and mainlining Christmas cookies during all that time she wasn't sleeping. In the background, I could see that the Christmas decorations we'd put up in the living room after Thanksgiving had been taken down. I added, "I handled it badly."

"You think?" she said, her face revealing the tiniest glimmer of humor. "If you didn't want to go to Barnard, why'd you even apply?"

"If you really want to know, I wasn't ready to make a decision about college at all last year. I only applied to Barnard because I was sure I wouldn't get in." My grades and test scores were good, but below the school's averages for its admitted candidates. It had been a calculated risk on my part, one I'd lost either because I was a legacy or because Dash helped me with my personal essay and edited it to perfection.

"Why didn't you just say that?"

"I didn't want to disappoint you."

"It's much more disappointing that you let us have the expectation you would go, when you had no intention to do so."

"I did intend to go."

Mom tried to smile. "Really?"

"I mean, theoretically, yes. I wanted to fulfill your college ambitions for me. Follow in your footsteps. Be closer to Grandpa. But it never felt like the right fit."

"So what is the right fit?"

"I'm still deciding. I guess that's what I wanted and didn't know how to tell you. I wanted the freedom to figure it out in my own time, in my own way."

"Fair enough. I'm sorry you're just telling me that now, but glad to know it."

"Don't freak out, but there's a dog school here in England I'm considering."

"Absolutely not."

"Mom." I paused, not just for dramatic effect, but also to gather my courage. "That's my decision to make. Not yours."

She made a surprised face. Then wiped a tear from her cheek. "Harsh, Lily."

"But I'd like you to help me make the decision," I added. "When I get home, I'll tell you more about it and you can see why it might be a great opportunity."

"To be near Dash?"

"That would just be a bonus. Not the reason." I took a deep breath and then said it. "I love him, Mom. I'm sorry you're not ready to let me go, but I'm ready to go. He's not just a big part of my life. He's the best part of it." I thought of this time last year, when I'd been a mess of insecurity because I didn't know where my relationship with Dash stood, if he really felt the same about me as I did about him, and now, a year later, it was a world of difference. I felt confident in my relationship and confident in myself in a way I never had before. Dash hadn't done that. *I* did it. By following my own path (and as many dogs as I could).

"I know, honey. It's that Dad and I want you to experience more on your own before you commit yourself to Dash."

"Too late. My heart landed on him. And it's not going anywhere."

The slow, single tear gave way to a gush. "Okay," Mom finally said. Or blubbered.

And now for the good news. I said, "I'm also going to apply to FIT."

She perked up as she wiped the tears from her face with a tissue. "Here in New York? Really?"

"Yes. I'm interested in design. And entrepreneurship. I think I might be good at both?"

"Something other than dogs! You don't know how relieved I am to hear you say that." *I do know,* I thought. *Thanks, Dashiell.*

"Where is my dog, by the way?" Mom turned her camera to her feet, where Boris's head was nestled, asleep. I couldn't believe it. If Mom "tolerated" Dash as my boyfriend, she blatantly "loathed" (her word, not mine) my ginormous dog. Or so I thought.

"We miss you," Mom said, turning the camera back on her sweet, tired face.

"I love you, Mom."

"I love you, too. Let's agree to talk things through more before making major decisions."

"Agreed. Please un-cancel Christmas," I said.

"Agreed. Come home already!"

I awoke the next morning, wishing for another vision of Dash in his purple pajamas. Then I remembered today was not only THE DAY BEFORE CHRISTMAS but also a big day for Dash. He wanted to cast his fate to books and today was his first big step in that direction, his interview with

214

what sounded like Sinjin Blakey someone-or-other. I was so excited for Dash and wondered if he'd opened my final Advent calendar gift to him yet. Dash wanted books? He'd get books.

The last present was a USB key with photos I'd taken in late October, when I'd gone on a day trip with my brother up to the Hudson Valley during peak fall foliage. We went to a glorious bookstore in Hillsdale, New York, called the Rodgers Book Barn, which was a rickety old country house filled with books, books, and more books, in every room, and outside on shelves. Langston photographed me holding many of Dash's favorite books under the gold-, yellow-, and red-covered trees, and hiding in the Book Barn's many reading nooks.

I opened my eyes. Alas, Dash was not standing at the window wearing purple pajamas, but luckily I had my photo of him doing so from the day before to brighten my morning. As I gazed at the photo, a text from Dash appeared.

I just opened your last Advent present. Sooooo many books.

I waited for him to tell me how awesome the present was. Nothing.

And? I finally typed back.

I think I'm having a panic attack, he answered.

sixteen

DASH

December 24th

'Twas the day before Christmas, and all through the flat came the cry "I DON'T KNOW WHAT TO WEAR!"

This was not a line I uttered with any frequency in my daily life. Most clothes, to me, were fairly interchangeable, as long as you put them on the part of the body they were meant to correspond with.

But an interview? With St. John Blakemore . . . aka SJB . . . aka one of the most high-powered literary editors in New York . . . aka (inexplicably) Gem's friend "Blakey"?

Gem came into my doorway.

"Goodness, you're just like your father!" she exclaimed.

I flinched, and she must have seen it, because she immediately amended, "Your father when he was in high school. Before he became . . . what he is today."

I had a hard time picturing my father in high school. My father never gave any indication that he'd once been young.

Gem, on the other hand, wore all of the ages she'd ever been at the same time. I could trust that.

"So what should I wear?" I asked her.

Gem smiled. "Whatever you think suits you. Don't be too formal. Just be yourself. That's what Blakey will want to see. Believe me, this interview will be about words, not clothes."

I bypassed the finery Gem had benefacted me and went with one of my favorite sweaters instead.

I would get this or lose this as myself, not some pretend version I thought someone else might want to see.

I do believe that most of the times your life changes, you don't realize in the moment that it's on the cusp of being altered. I can't remember the last family outing we had before my parents decided to split. I had no idea spotting a flash of red on the shelves of the Strand would lead me to Lily. It would have been impossible to figure that receiving a sweatshirt in the post would lead to my greatest academic miscalculation.

But sometimes, just sometimes, there are moments that feel like an appointment with the future. Fate stops being a wind and takes the shape of a flight path.

This was one of those moments: standing outside the Blakemores' town house, deciding whether to use the knocker or ring the bell.

I opted for the knocker.

The footsteps I heard behind the wood door were much slower than my heartbeat. Then the door opened, and I faced . . .

Sir Ian?

"Oh," he said, equally surprised. "It's *you*." Then he gave me a camaraderie-tinged smile. "It makes perfect sense, in a way. Who better for Uncle SJB to interrupt our Christmas to see?"

He ushered me inside and offered to take my coat. As I passed it over to him, I asked, "You call him Uncle SJB?"

"Yes, Salinger," Sir Ian replied. "But I'm the only one who does. I don't suggest you call him that."

Much to my horror, it was starting again. The walls of my skull pushing on my brain. Thoughts dizzying to a degree they threatened to lose their ability to speak.

Sir Ian touched me lightly on the shoulder.

"Breathe," he said.

I nodded, breathed.

Sir Ian continued, "Don't call him Uncle SJB . . . but think of him that way. I know you must envision him as a knight of the royal order of editors, but he also keeps a rubber ducky on the side of his tub in his bathroom here. He's allergic to chocolate and tries to eat it anyway. He has published some of the greatest authors of our time, but he's also missed the chance to publish some of the greatest authors of our time. He lost his first love when she fell for a zoologist. He has yogurt for breakfast every morning. On mornings when he really wants to treat himself, he might add berries."

"Why are you telling me all this?"

"To remind you he's human. And to make sure you don't bring up zoology."

"Thank you."

"Anything to help a fellow Oxford escapee get to where he wants to be. Now come this way—I believe he's in the parlor."

It was only a few steps away, behind another old wooden door.

"Here we go," Sir Ian said, opening it with a flourish.

Deep breath.

Appointment with the future.

I stepped inside, and for a moment I thought Sir Ian was going to follow. But instead he said, "Good luck," and winked at me. Then he flourished again and left me in the parlor, where a man with salt-and-pepper hair was standing up from an armchair, grinning at me.

"So here he is!" the most famous literary editor in New York proclaimed in his high London accent. "The legendary American grandson!"

And I was so flustered that I replied, "Uncle SJB!"

Before I could dissolve into a pool of mortification, he laughed and shook my hand.

"I feel closer to Gemma than I do to most of my family, so that makes a certain amount of sense. We like to joke that we swapped lives so I could take Manhattan and she could be the toast of London Town. Here, sit."

He gestured to a settee across from the armchair. I tried to set myself in the settee with maximum grace, but the settee was set against that and made me wobble when I would have preferred to casually recline.

SJB launched into our interview as soon as his arm hit the armrest of the armchair. "So here's the thing," he said. "Gemma explained where you are, and I am sympathetic to your situation. I'm not sure if you knew my wayward nephew in your Oxford months, but a case such as yours recently hit our family, and I was decidedly a defender, not a member of the prosecution. If ever asked, I am sure to say that I was wooed away from this country—when in reality, it was much more like a prison break. Nothing against the old Queen, but she and I were never a good fit. And as such, I must warn you that I am not a fan of riding on your old family name. Gemma's recommendation got you in the door, but it will not get you anywhere else on its own accord. I owe her many, many times over, but I don't owe anyone enough to compromise my professionalism. Is that understood?"

I nodded.

"Good. So now tell me—why are you here?"

I could feel my heart racing, and couldn't believe that he couldn't feel it, too. It was such a simple question. But there wasn't a simple answer.

I just had to start at the center of it.

"I love books," I said.

I couldn't stop there. It wasn't enough.

"I have always loved books," I went on. "And I am sure with every ounce of my being that I will always love books. And I am in the rare and privileged position right now to be able to ask myself what I love, and to see if I can make a future that walks beside the things I love. I had thought, in going to Oxford, that what I wanted to do was study books, pin their pages to the bulletin board like a butterfly collector and analyze the patterns in their wings. But I realized—that wasn't it. And while I feel extraordinarily satisfied when I find the right word for the right occasion, I don't think my future lies in being an author. No. I don't want to be the creator or the scientist. I want to be the shepherd, the person who knows books so well that he can help make books even better than they were when they came out of the author's mind. Because, at heart, when I tell you I love books, what I am telling you is that I am a reader. Boil off all my pretensions, let my attempts at erudition rise away from me like steam, and what would be left would be a reader who is frequently amazed and educated by what words can do on a page. That's why I'm here. Because I have never, ever met another person who felt the same way. And now, here you are, across from me. Which is, frankly, terrifying."

SJB leaned back in his chair and really looked at me for what felt like a terrifyingly long time but may have only been a second or two.

Finally, he said, "Tell me about a book you've read lately that you think everyone should read. Don't overthink it—first thought, best thought."

"There's this book called *Kent State* by Deborah Wiles—have you read it?"

He shook his head.

"But you know about Kent State, right?"

"Four American students killed by the National Guard in 1970, correct?"

"Exactly. Before I graduated high school, my English teacher, Ms. Cameron-Ryan, gave me a list of books to read over the summer, and *Kent State* was at the top of it. It's not really fiction and it's not really nonfiction—it's all of these voices telling the story of what happened, from different vantage points. And the thing is, you know what happened. You know from the start that four students died. But even though you know where it's going, as the book goes on, you fill with more and more despair, hoping it won't happen. Because you realize that these four students died because of adults, because of a long tradition of American hostility and injustice. And they were my age, right? Some of them were just walking to class. And then their own armed forces, the people who were supposed to be protecting them, open fire. It's devastating. And some of the National Guardsmen? They were the same age as the students. And you see how they were all trapped in that moment, and as a reader, you are trapped there with them. Which is what a great book does, right? It traps you into feeling something important. Whether it's about yourself, or society, or ideally both. I think about it a lot, especially how they were my age, and became frozen in time. How wrong that is. You really need to read it."

"I will," SJB said. "Maybe you can bring me a copy when you start."

"Start?"

"Interning for me."

"Wait—that's the whole interview?"

SJB smiled again. "Absolutely. When you're interviewing someone for an editorial position, those are really the only two questions you need to ask. When I'm in the office, I sometimes pad it with other questions to make Human Resources happy, but at the end of the day, if you have the right reason for being here and you know how to connect with a book and pass that connection on to someone else—that's all I really need to know."

"Okay," I said. "I mean, thank you. Thank you so much."

"So you'll be back in New York after the holidays are over? I'm back the first full week of January. So maybe come in that Friday and we'll figure out the days you can come each week?"

I didn't even have to think about it.

"That sounds perfect," I said.

Because even though he was saying it as a question, it came across to me as an answer. I *was* going back to New York. I *was* going to start working as his intern. I doubted it was full-time, and I doubted it would pay a lot, if at all. But I would take on other jobs if I had to. I'd go back to living with my mom. I would see about transferring out of Oxford—to Columbia or anywhere else in New York that would take me.

Lily and I would be in the same city again. We'd build our lives together. Which was the first step to building a life together.

That felt right. It all felt right.

SJB and I talked some more—him asking me about Gem and what I'd been up to in London, me asking him about what he was working on and what the family's Christmas Eve plans were. Even though I had gotten the job (it seemed? right?), I still wanted to make a good impression. But my head was spinning so much that none of the words were really landing.

Finally, SJB stood from his armchair and said he had to go do some last-minute gift wrapping. Which was a good thing, because one word finally landed: *gifts*.

Somehow, with everything going on, I had forgotten to buy anyone Christmas gifts.

SJB walked me out into the main hallway. Sir Ian was soon there, too, holding my coat. SJB told me he'd email Gem with all the details, including his assistant's contact information, since she'd "set everything up." Then he shook my hand again and went upstairs.

Sir Ian raised an eyebrow. "By Jove, Salinger," he said, "I think you got it."

"I did," I said, not trying to hide the disbelief in my voice. "I really think I got it."

"I'd have to pull a Harry-and-Meghan and officially remove myself from this family in order to get an internship through him . . . so I can truly say it couldn't have happened to a better gent."

"And what'll you do?" I asked. "Assuming you're not going back to Oxford."

"I think it would take a dæmon to drag me back to Oxford. My fallback was to study the Knowledge full-time— you know, the test they give people who want to be London cabbies, proving they've gotten the whole city memorized. I don't necessarily want to drive a cab, but I'd love to be able to say I passed the test. Or perhaps I might learn more at another university. In the meantime, I threw myself on the mercy of Foyles, and they were kind enough to install me in the home office. I may get myself into publishing yet. Just not through the family entrance."

"Hey," I told him, "just be grateful that you have a family that treasures books. My mom likes them in theory but never has time to read them. And my dad is the guy who will only pick up a book if it has the word *wealth* in the title."

"I shiver at the thought."

"He cringes at me, I cringe at him—it's a great relationship."

"If you can believe it, my father isn't much better. But the rest of my family has its compensations."

"Yeah," I said, thinking of Gem, "mine does, too."

Sir Ian offered my coat out to me. "I don't mean to chase you off," he said. "If you'd like to stay for some eggnog, I'm sure I could whip some up."

"No," I replied, "I should be going. I have to buy some gifts before the shops close."

Sir Ian looked at his watch. "Cutting it close, surely?"

I shrugged. "'Tis the season."

Sir Ian told me he'd no doubt wrangle a visit to New York at some point in the year, so hopefully our paths would cross again. I told him I'd like that.

"Thanks," I said. "For telling me to breathe. And for the other night."

"To be the right person at the right time for someone else is the highest service we can perform," Sir Ian said with a bow. "Now go get some presents."

As soon as I was back on the street, I checked my phone. I only had a couple of hours to get my gifts. For Lily. For Gem. For my mom, who I'd be seeing sooner than she knew. Even one for Mrs. Basil E. I wanted them to be special. So special. Marking not just Christmas, but the start of the next chapter. The Oxford chapter had been a short one.

But the next one?

Already I felt it might last much longer.

seventeen

LiLY

December 24th

I had all the Christmas presents I'd ever need right in front of me.

While Dash went for his interview, I stood in the middle of a dog run at a local rescue organization just outside Twickenham, in the company of a pack of dogs, all of them very good boys and girls. The dogs were getting their outdoor time before returning to their kennels, where they'd dream about their future furever homes. They were all mixes, but observing their dominant characteristics, I counted two Staffies, one beagle, four terriers, one shar-pei, one West Highland white terrier whom I'd specifically come to meet to potentially match with Gem, and one black whippet/Labrador mix who had other ideas.

"I think she likes you," Jane Douglas said to me as a divine pup—tall, with a short black coat, a thick white stripe running from her neck to the top of her belly, and the sweetest and most soulful brown eyes—parked herself at my feet.

I wanted to say, *Well, pretty much all dogs like me,* but I knew stone-faced Jane Douglas would not appreciate my playful American boasting. The other dogs ran rampant, chasing Frisbees and birds and each other, but this Whipador only wanted to press herself against my ankles. "What's her name?" I asked.

"Asta. She's been here for over a year now, with no takers. She's a good girl, but terribly shy. She doesn't put on the 'Please like me' show that gets dogs adopted the quickest."

"How old?"

"We think about eight. She's very smart, gentle, gets on with other dogs but doesn't seek out their companionship. She'd probably do best in a home with no other pets. She's a bit anxious, so she'll need someone who'll be patient with her, preferably someone who doesn't work long hours away from the house. She's the kind of dog who just wants a book and her human—whoever that may be. Who were you thinking?"

"My boyfriend's grandmother. She lives in London. She meets all those requirements—and she loves a good book, like her grandson." Gem was totally Asta's human. I could feel it in my cold winter bones and warm dog heart.

I smiled, but Jane Douglas's face remained stern. "I hope you weren't thinking to give a dog as a Christmas gift."

"Never!" I was offended just by the suggestion. Pets needed time, love, and loads of attention to adapt to their new home environments. Christmas, with all its distractions, was the worst day of the year to make that connection. "I'm going to take some video of Asta and try to talk Gem—that's my boyfriend's grandmother—into coming to meet Asta after the holidays. Do you think Asta will still be here then?"

"I could almost guarantee it. So, tell me, Lily. Have you decided if you'll be joining us at PCFI next term? I have a waiting list of candidates eager to hear from me should you decide to give up your spot. The deadline for your decision isn't for another two weeks, but if you know, you know."

I knew I wanted the kind of education PCFI could provide. But despite assuring my family I wouldn't make a decision based on my boyfriend, the truth was, I couldn't see myself at PCFI if Dash wasn't also in England. And looking around at the dogs frolicking in the dog run, I grieved the idea of leaving my New York pack of dogs. At the same time, I loved the idea of immersing myself for a year in All Things Dog in my new favorite country across the pond.

"I'm considering how I could make it work," I said. *How I could do it without my family disowning me*, I thought. "I also have a dog crafts business. I'd have to figure out how to do that from here—like, getting materials, finding a work space for crafting, learning UK shipping rules."

"Problem solved," said Jane Douglas. "You won't have time for that during your year at PCFI. It's a full-time commitment. You'll either be studying or working here at the rescue center. In fact, I could use more volunteers right now. The Canine Supporters World Education Conference starts next week, and we need all hands on deck to prepare. Can I count you in?"

But . . .

"It's Christmas Eve," I reminded her.

"I'm aware. And appalled by how many volunteers opted out of helping today and tomorrow. They call themselves dog people. Rubbish."

One of those volunteers who hadn't dared take off on Christmas Eve approached Jane Douglas. "They need you inside," he told her. "Catering decision."

"For the dogs or the humans?" she asked.

"The humans."

"Nonsense," she huffed, and returned indoors.

"She's a charmer, right?" said the volunteer, a twenty-something guy with a hipster beard. He peered more closely at me and then said, "You're Lily, the dog-walker rock star!"

"I'm Lily," I affirmed. "Dog lover, not a rock star."

"I owe you a big thank-you," he said, extending his hand for me to shake. "I'm Albert. I just graduated from PCFI."

I shook his hand. "You don't need to thank me for that."

He laughed. "Good thing, because I worked my arse off the last year. No, I'm thanking you because I got a job through your referral."

"How's that possible?" I was good with dogs, but I couldn't magically provide employment to cynophilists, the fancy word for dog fanciers. My heart skipped a beat thinking how much Dash would like that word.

Albert said, "That dog you helped on the set of *The Thames of Our Lives?*"

"Daisy?"

"Daisy! You gave the producer Jane Douglas's number for a referral for a proper trainer. Jane referred me for the job. I can afford Christmas now!" Perhaps I was a little magical? Maybe some American boasting wasn't unreasonable? Albert's smile disappeared. "Except I'll be working here on Christmas."

I said, "I'm sure there'll be plenty of time to spend your earnings after Christmas. Plus, things will be on sale."

"I can afford my rent next month now. That's Christmas present enough." He noticed Asta at my feet. "I see you've made a friend. And the toughest one of the bunch."

"I'm going to try to convince my boyfriend's grandmother to adopt her after the holidays."

"I'll do my best to make sure Asta remains available till then." Albert crouched down to give Asta a good belly rub. "Are you Lily's groupie?" he asked Asta. That did it. Asta and Gem, a former groupie, were clearly soul mates.

I sat down on the ground to give Asta more attention as well. While I petted her, I asked Albert, "So what did you think of PCFI? I'm deciding whether to go."

"You won't find a better program or teacher in the world," said Albert. "But be prepared. Jane Douglas lives for dogs, and she expects her students to as well. She doesn't have a partner and she doesn't get on with her children, so all her attention is focused on her canine family. She lives and breathes dogs one hundred and ten percent of the time."

I understood better why my parents, and Dash, were concerned that my love for dogs bordered on too much. They wanted me to have more in my life.

I thought of Gem asking Dash what he wanted to do—his heart's answer. I asked mine the same. Its response was immediate and certain.

Yes, I wanted to work with dogs—but not to the exclusion of my family, my love, and my other interests, like design and growing a business.

Regardless of where Dash chose to be, I belonged in New York right now. I wanted to be near my family, in all their suffocating glory, and with my glorious dog, Boris, and my best-in-show dog-walking charges. I wanted to grow my business there. I wanted to go back to school to support all those things, but not leave Manhattan to do so.

I probably knew all that from the second I discovered that the classroom was in Jane Douglas's living room, but now I definitely knew. PCFI was not the place for me.

I was ready to go home. My future was there.

And so was Dash's!

Dash, Gem, and I celebrated at Gem's house with a traditional British Christmas dinner a day early, as we'd all be flying back to New York early on Christmas morning. The dining room was lit with candles and decorated with holly boughs. Stevie Wonder's "Someday at Christmas" played from a speaker connected to a playlist on Gem's phone.

Gem raised her glass for a toast. "Here's to Dash's future in publishing," she said.

"And to Lily's future as a dogpreneur," Dash said.

"And to Gem's future as Asta's greatest human ever," I said.

We clinked glasses. Then Gem said, "I didn't say yes, dear Lily."

"Let's look at the video of Asta playing fetch again?" I suggested. Gem had gotten used to Dash's company in London. Once he was back in New York, Asta would be the best antidote to missing him, just like Boris had been for me.

"I'll think about it," said Gem. That was as good as a yes, in my experience. The people who were No's were adamant about that from the get-go. The prospective adopters who said *I'll think about it* almost always turned to the Yes camp. They just needed a little time to get used to the idea. I predicted that within a month, Asta would be lying in her dog bed by the fire while—or "whilst," as the Brits say—Gem reorganized her massive vinyl collection in order of the music Asta responded to best. Such a good girl, that Asta!

"Let's eat," said Dash.

"First, the bangers," said Gem. From her plate, she lifted a gift-wrapped tube, tied in the middle with Christmas ribbon and twisted at the ends, and gestured for us to do the same with the tubes on our own plates. "These are Christmas crackers, also called bangers. They get opened before the Christmas meal. Hold your cracker in your right hand, then we'll cross our arms and pull apart each other's crackers from the left."

We assumed the formation and pulled. The tubes made a *BANG* as their contents spilled out onto the dinner table: a few small cards, some confetti, and folded pieces of tissue paper.

Gem reached for one of the cards. "Terrible joke time!" She read her card aloud. "Why are pirates great?" Dash and I shrugged. Gem said, "They just aaaaaaarrrrr!"

"Groan," said Dash.

"Applause," I enthused.

"I'm going to post that one to Johnny Depp in a Christmas card," said Gem. "We spent a week together on his yacht, back when he had one. Not that I signed an NDA for a memoir of his that never got published."

"Of course you didn't," said Dash. He turned to me. "What's yours say?"

I reached for the card from my Christmas cracker. "What did the sea say to Santa? Nothing! It just waved!"

Dash shook his head disdainfully.

Gem said, "How about yours, Dash?"

He read his card aloud. "What do you call Santa's little helpers? Subordinate Clauses!" He sighed. I clapped for real this time.

"And now for *The Crown*," said Gem.

"Oh, no!" I said. "I'd love to stay and watch, but I promised my aunt we'd go see her after dinner."

"Not that crown," said Gem. She took the folded pieces of tissue paper that came out of the bangers and passed them to me and Dash, then demonstrated with her own, unfolding it and placing it on her head. It was shaped like a crown. "It's British tradition to wear a paper crown at Christmas dinner."

Dash said, "This country prides itself on pomp and circumstance, yet spends its Christmas telling terrible jokes that come from something called bangers, along with wearing crowns crafted from flimsy tissue paper. Not dignified at all."

I placed my paper crown on my head. "Pip pip, guvnah. I love it."

Dash did the same with his pink crown. He could only have looked more handsome if he'd also been wearing his purple silk pajamas.

My stomach churned in delight as my eyes took in the meal on the table. Gem had made a meatless lentil roast in my honor, as well as British staples like carrots and peas, roast potatoes and parsnips, brussels sprouts, and a thick, creamy concoction called bread sauce to go with it all.

"Do we say grace first?" I asked.

"Do we?" said Gem, alarmed.

"Grace," said Dash.

Gem laughed. "Would you like to say grace, Lily?"

I did. I said, "I would just like to say how happy I am to be here and how happy I am that you and Dash have each other. Amen."

"That's lovely," said Gem. "Thank you. I feel the same."

My graceful lead-in accomplished, I added, "And I've been so distracted from being here and making all these big life decisions that I forgot to buy Christmas presents."

It was true. The Queen of Christmas had forgotten the whole reason for the season. STUFF.

Gem said, "I mean this sincerely despite how trite it may sound: You both being here now is present enough for me."

Dash looked at me, full of love, and took my hand in his. "Lily, I also mean this sincerely. You should have gotten me a present." I dropped his hand. He laughed, then turned serious. "I felt lost when you arrived. I wasn't sure I wanted you to be here. Not because I didn't want to see you—I longed to see you—but because I didn't want you to see me feeling so defeated by my own ambitions. But you came anyway, and I love you for that. And I love you for figuring out what you want and having the confidence to achieve it. You've inspired me to do the same. I'd say that's gift enough. *You* are grace."

Gem dabbed a tiny tear from the corner of her eye. "Honestly, Dash. I have no idea where you learned how to be in a healthy and happy relationship. You had no examples."

"Books," he said.

I a little bit wanted to cry, too, but instead I asked Dash, "But seriously. What did you get me?"

Dash flashed me his rare smile that melts me. "You'll have to wait to find out."

As Gem started passing the food around, she said, "Speaking of gifts . . . in honor of your British Christmas, I'm sending you back to your hotel with some Christmas stockings and treats. In Britain, you leave the stockings over your bed instead of over the fireplace, along with a plate of mince pies for Father Christmas."

I didn't know what mince pies were, but if they were as awful as they sounded (like chopped mice), maybe they'd give the big guy a jump start on his New Year's diet.

Dash said, "So Father Christmas basically stalks kids in their sleep on Christmas Eve? No wonder the Brits don't leave him cookies. He doesn't deserve them."

I *never* would have been able to sleep on Christmas Eve as a kid if I knew Santa might be coming into my room to leave gifts in my stocking. I had so much to talk to him about.

Tiny tots with their eyes all aglow
Will find it hard to sleep tonight.

"The Christmas Song" was the next song on Gem's playlist. The singer sounded vaguely familiar, but I couldn't recall hearing this version of the song before. Dash listened intently. "Is that . . . Barbra Streisand?"

"Correct," said Gem. "Her Christmas album is one of the best-selling Christmas albums ever."

"But she's Jewish," said Dash.

Gem said, "So is Irving Berlin, who wrote 'White Christmas.' So is Kenny G, who by the way put out the best-selling Christmas album of all time after Elvis."

Dash said, "Please tell me Kenny G isn't next on your playlist."

I said, "Please tell me Elvis is!"

We dug into the food. Gem turned out to be a much better cook than she was a baker. "Delicious," I told Gem as I happily ate the lentil loaf, which was even more delicious slathered with Tesco brand vegan bread sauce, which was like gravy, but without animals suffering to make it. The bread sauce was particularly delicious on the roast potatoes, which made me all the more excited for tomorrow night's Christmas snack: latkes. Since Langston would be at his boyfriend's, and Mrs. Basil E.'s big Christmas night party was canceled, my mom had messaged me that we'd be having a Jewish Christmas this year. While Dash went off with Gem to see their own family, my family would be going out for Chinese food, then a movie, *Cyborg Santa;* Mom said she was excited to see artificial intelligence destroy the capitalist patriarchy. We'd enjoy some latkes once we got back home. I couldn't wait. A new tradition?

Aha! I could gift everyone online with Christmas albums by Jews! Shopping DONE! Thanks for the inspo, Babs.

I was used to Christmas Eves that passed with almost unbearable excitement and anticipation. Gem's celebration felt so . . . *grown-up.* Civilized, unchaotic, gracious, sophisticated. Exactly the opposite of the Christmas Eves of my childhood. Not better—not worse: different. I loved it. We talked about books and music and Dash's future in publishing and mine with dogs and the music Gem would listen to with Asta while reading books.

After the meal ended and we'd cleared the table of the dinner food, Gem announced, "And now, for your Christmas surprise." I half expected Father Christmas to come charging in to beg us to place our stockings over a fireplace because he didn't want to disturb our sleep and the sugarplums dancing in our heads. After a dramatic pause, Gem said, with great pride, "We'll be having dessert!"

Dash said, "I hate to break this to you, Gem, but dessert at the end of a meal is not a surprise."

"This one will be," said Gem. "Because it involves fire."

She went to the kitchen and returned carrying a metal plate with what looked like a dome-shaped fruitcake on it, a holly sprig decorating the top. "Someone please turn the lights out," she said.

Dash got up and turned off the lights. The candles now solely lit the room, making it feel even more cozy. Sorry, cosy. Gem placed the cake plate on the table. "This is what the Brits call Christmas pudding. It's a fruitcake, but not like the terrible ones in America. Christmas pudding is made with dried fruit and soaked in alcohol over a period of months so it's ready to set fire to and then eat at Christmas dinner."

She picked up a metal spoon and poured some brandy into it. With her other hand, she picked up a lighter.

Dash said, "A fruitcake that doesn't taste terrible and might intoxicate us will indeed be a surprise."

Gem said, "No, the surprise will be if I manage not to burn the house down. The last time I tried this, your father was about ten years old. I forgot to remove the holly sprig first and it caught fire along with the cake. A flame flew out from it and set his dinner tie on fire. He'd been so stubborn about putting that tie on, and then that happened. He was fine, we got the fire out quickly, but his eyebrow got singed, and I don't think he ever forgave me." She took a deep breath. "Here we go. Let's try this again."

Dash tactfully removed the holly sprig that Gem had once again forgotten to set aside.

As she lit the alcohol in the spoon, her face aglow with a mixture of fear and glee, I admired her courage. She was trying to set a cake on fire, and she was going to attempt to reconcile with her son on Christmas. The latter would be riskier than the former.

The spoon on fire, Gem then poured the flaming liquid over the cake, which turned a magnificent bluish yellow before the flame died out. The cake was blackened and looked about as appetizing as I imagined mince pies to be.

"You did it," Dash proudly told his grandmother.

"I did it," she murmured.

"We look so fine in our finery," I whispered into Dash's ear. We wore the elegant clothes that Gem had gotten us from Liberty, Dash in a nice suit and tie and me in a red, ruffled, sequin-embellished minidress with a high neck, long sleeves, and a wickedly short pleated skirt.

He held me close. "Father Christmas is scandalized by the length—or lack thereof—of that dress. Very, very naughty."

"Does he like it, though?"

Dash kissed me in response. "He *loves* it. But don't tell

Mrs. Claus. I mean, Mrs. Father Christmas? Who's Santa's wife in England?"

I laughed. "Admit it. You love Christmas."

"I love Christmas when *you* are part of it."

We were alone outside on the balcony of Mrs. Basil E.'s Grand Piano Suite, while inside, Mrs. Basil E. had another rager of a holiday party happening. I wasn't surprised she had that many friends in London, but I was impressed how many made themselves available for an impromptu Christmas Eve gathering. There were at least two dozen people, drinking and eating and laughing, my favorite kind of merrymaking on my favorite eve of merry. Mark played Christmas carols at the piano while Julia, Mrs. Basil E., and Gem sang along with him. In a corner, Azra Khatun and some guy called Sir Ian were deep in conversation. Next to the piano sat the unwon Daunt Books Bibliophile Cup, which Mark hoped Claridge's would accept as a new piece of artwork for the Grand Piano Suite.

Dash held me from behind as we looked outward over the London cityscape. We had dear friends and relations, old and new, here. We'd come back to London a lot more, I hoped.

In just a few hours, we'd be on our way back to New York. Dash would be returning home, but his journey in his old place would be just beginning. Mine, too.

"Merry Christmas," I told Dash.

"Happy Chrimbo," he said.

I felt so lucky.

I felt so loved.

eighteen

DASH

December 25th

I was walking through Mayfair when it caught my eye. Window after window of Christmas decorations had left me eyesore. So I needed a spot of calm, apart from the tinsel and the glare. I had stopped looking . . . and that's when I saw it.

It was a glass dove, no bigger than my hand. Its wings were wide, its direction clear. I went inside the store and asked to see it. It was exactly what I'd been looking for—beautifully regal and beautifully imperfect, frozen in a moment, but still clearly in the middle of flight; solid and weighty, but also fragile, breakable; it would stay safe as long as you took care of it.

It cost much more than I could spare. But I got it anyway.

I gave it to her as the minute hand brought us past midnight, the start of our thirty-hour Christmas Day.

We would not have to wait for Santa; we had our own sleigh, which took the form of a bed in a posh hotel in the middle of London. This was where the reindeer had brought us before leaving to do their own thing. After an evening of everyone else, it was now just the two of us: Lily in an oversize silk pajama top, me in the corresponding bottoms. Together we made quite a pair.

I brought the present over to our sleigh, and she took off its wrappings gently, as if she were taking off its coat. When she opened the box itself, I saw that it wasn't what she was expecting . . . but it also was exactly what she wanted. In the soft blue darkness of the hotel room, it nearly hovered from her hand, part sculpture, part air.

"I love her," Lily said.

And I said, "I do, too."

I cued up Ella Fitzgerald's "Have Yourself a Merry Little Christmas" and her voice filled the room as we held each other in our sleigh, the delicate, brave bird nestled between us. Here we were, heartbeats and darkness and breath and wings and glass and love and music and nowhere else in the world we wanted to be. Here we were, and here we'd be, until we stepped off our sleigh and traded it for a plane. And what I felt was so unexpected and so important that I had to say it out loud.

"I'm excited for the future," I told Lily. "I'm really, really excited."

"Me too," she replied.

And in that moment, there wasn't any fear. There wasn't

any hesitation. There wasn't even the constant voice of uncertainty. There was only togetherness. There was only excitement. There was only love.

"Here's to the future," Lily said. "A wonderful future."

And I believed.

ACKNOWLEDGMENTS

Thank you, as always, to our friends, family members, and readers, for bringing us joy, even when it's not a holiday season.

Thanks, too, to our wonderful editor, Nancy Hinkel, as well as Melanie Nolan, Barbara Marcus, Mary McCue, and everyone else at Random House Children's Books. Much gratitude as well to our publishers outside the US and to our agents and all of the people at the Clegg Agency and WME.

In a very strange serendipity of timing, this book was written in part while the first season of the *Dash & Lily* TV series was filmed. (One chapter was even written while David sat on the floor of the Rare Book Room in the Strand at three in the morning, watching the final scene of the series come to life.) So thank you to Joe Tracz, Scott Hedley, the D&L writers room team, everyone at 21 Laps, everyone at Netflix, the three directors, and the perfect cast, particularly Midori Francis and Austin Abrams. We hope you all get a trip to London out of this one. (Take us with you.)